# TSUNAMI

### RACHEL HATCH
BOOK 9

## L.T. RYAN

with
### BRIAN SHEA

LIQUID MIND MEDIA

Copyright © 2022 by L.T. Ryan, Liquid Mind Media, LLC, & Brian Christopher Shea. All rights reserved. No part of this publication may be copied, reproduced in any format, by any means, electronic or otherwise, without prior consent from the copyright owner and publisher of this book. This is a work of fiction. All characters, names, places and events are the product of the author's imagination or used fictitiously. For information contact:

contact@ltryan.com

http://LTRyan.com

https://www.facebook.com/JackNobleBooks

# THE RACHEL HATCH SERIES

Drift

Downburst

Fever Burn

Smoke Signal

Firewalk

Whitewater

Aftershock

Whirlwind

Tsunami

Fastrope

*Sidewinder (Coming Soon)*

RACHEL HATCH SHORT STORIES

Fractured

Proving Ground

The Gauntlet

Join the LT Ryan reader family & receive a free copy of the Rachel Hatch story, Fractured. Click the link below to get started:

https://ltryan.com/rachel-hatch-newsletter-signup-1

**Love Hatch? Noble? Maddie? Cassie?** Get your very own Jack Noble merchandise today! Click the link below to find coffee mugs, t-shirts, and even signed copies of your favorite L.T. Ryan thrillers! https://ltryan.ink/EvG_

# ONE

Digging the hole was hard enough. Knowing what it was for, made it that much worse.

Tyler Pierce jammed the shovel into the soft, wet earth and had long since given up counting the passage of time.

The hole was just shy of three feet deep now. A layer of water coated the exposed ground around his boots. Leaning his arm against the shovel handle, he ran a muddy hand across his brow. Light rain had mixed with his perspiration while headlights slashed through the water falling from the sky, giving it a strobe effect. He squinted against the light. Through the mud-covered veil of his hand, Tyler looked up from the hole to see Quinn Russell's smug face. It was the same look he'd had on his face every time he'd looked up at the man who'd ordered him to dig.

Tyler had only agreed to meet Quinn tonight hoping to see Quinn's sister Max. She didn't show. That left Quinn and Tyler out here in the middle of the night, one digging a hole, the other watching impatiently.

And then there was the third guy, duct taped in the lawn chair next to Quinn.

Tyler knew this was bad, but he knew it was worse to cross Quinn. His feelings for Max were strong. His fear of Quinn was stronger. To say the ex-con had a hot temper was an understatement. And although Quinn had sworn he'd changed his ways, the circumstances Tyler now faced proved he hadn't, in fact, changed one bit. If anything, the circumstances added to the man's criminal resume–kidnapping, arson, armed robbery, and whatever this hole would end up being.

Tyler wouldn't allow himself to imagine what would happen after he stopped digging. It's why he'd begun taking more frequent breaks, hoping Quinn would tell him to stop. But Tyler's slow progression had done nothing but worsen Quinn's already sour mood. And even in trying not to think about it, Tyler knew very well what this hole was for. The shape of it lay six feet long by three feet wide. And a depth of three feet, thanks to Tyler's plodding effort. It was enough room for the man in the chair. Still, Tyler couldn't help but hope this was something else. A threat or just a game.

Anything other than the truth.

Tyler rested the shovel against the edge of the pit and wiped his hands down the front of his jeans. His palms and fingers burned from the hours of gripping the wooden handle and forcing the shovel in and out of the ground. His palms stung, the blisters already forming.

The captive's pleas had dropped to a low whimper, his strength waning. But the man's first shrill, desperate cries for help against layers of duct tape was a sound Tyler would hear long after this night was over.

Tyler blinked sweat and tears from his eyes as he looked up at Quinn. "I don't think I'll be able to muscle out another three feet deep. The ground's too wet. Too heavy. Gonna take me twice as long as the first half." He stuck the shovel's tip into the muck to stress the point. None of his attempts, subtle or otherwise, seemed to find their intended mark.

Quinn shrugged then turned his attention to his prisoner. "Then I suppose three feet will have to do."

With that, Tyler tossed the shovel out of the hole and climbed out, slipping on the muddy edge. He avoided eye contact with the man in the chair. It was bad enough he'd be haunted by that scream. He didn't need to add in the tortured eyes of the condemned man. Instead, Tyler focused his gaze elsewhere. His stomach dropped at the devious smile appearing on Quinn's face.

"Tyler, meet Frank Dibner." Quinn was more animated than normal. A big smile on his face.

It was obvious Tyler was supposed to know the name, so he racked his brain trying to place the name with the face. Neither stuck. Quinn talked a lot about the monsters behind the world's climate crisis, but Tyler couldn't recall the name Frank Dibner. He knew Quinn well enough to know the environment was just another fight he could pick. Another outlet for his rage. But Tyler knew the one thing that motivated him more than anything else. Money.

Dibner squeaked something indecipherable through the duct tape.

Tyler couldn't bring himself to look at the captive. "I should really get going." He hoped to distance himself from whatever this was. He was angry at himself for being sucked into it. And even angrier knowing that if Max sent another message, he would do it all again.

After another restrained whimper, Tyler steeled himself and turned to face the man in the chair. He took a moment to study him. Tyler guessed Dibner to be in his late 50s, early 60s. His gray hair was matted over his face from the rain. He wore a high-quality blazer and button-down shirt. His wristwatch spoke of money, and Tyler couldn't help but think that somebody, somewhere, would be looking for this man. When it came to victims with money, people usually didn't stop looking.

Tyler knew the hole he'd dug could only be used for one thing, yet he couldn't stop himself from hoping it was an elaborate ruse. But when he looked back from Dibner's desperate eyes to Quinn Russell, he saw nothing but resolve in his *associate*.

"Frank here has brutally damaged our environment." Quinn placed his hand on Dibner's shoulder. "Isn't that right, Frankie?"

Dibner let his gaze fall to the grave.

Quinn stuck his smug face in front of Dibner's, blocking the view. Fairhaven's early fall always brought with it a coolness to the nighttime air, and Quinn's breath danced around the other man's visage as Quinn lowered himself to a squat.

"You've done a damn fine job over the last forty years of destroying our environment. You may not care because the clock is ticking, and the sands of your hourglass are coming to an end. But in the wake of your life and your business, you have devastated our world and doomed it to hell."

Quinn rose, a silhouette against the moon, which broke through the racing storm clouds.

"A quick Google search will show that Frank is leading the charge on alternative energy, that he's now a big partner of Aurora Nuclear, a shift to a cleaner energy source from the crude oil that made him billions. But don't let him fool you. If you dig deep enough, you'll find out why." Quinn glowered down at Dibner. "Frank, would you like to tell our young friend here the real reason you decided to switch to clean energy? Why you saw nuclear power as an alternative to the oil that built your empire?"

Dibner tried to speak, but again the words were muffled in his throat.

Without warning, Quinn ripped the duct tape from Dibner's mouth. The man howled in pain. His expression shifted from worry to rage. He flailed against the restraints holding him against the chair and spat at Quinn. The projected saliva was knocked off target by the rain as it increased in intensity, washing out the sounds of his primal scream.

Quinn pulled out a roll of duct tape and held a finger to his lips. "Your screaming won't matter out here. Nobody will hear you. Especially not on a rainy night." Lightning lit up the sky and thunder crashed a moment later. All three men flinched. The smile returned to Quinn's face for a moment. "But I can't take any chances. Open your mouth and scream again, and the tape goes back on. And the next time it does, it's never coming off."

Dibner cursed Quinn in a tone barely audible through the rain.

"Now that we have an understanding, why don't you explain yourself?"

Dibner licked the rain off his upper lip. "It's the future. It's going to be our way back. It will fill the void and limit our dependency on fossil fuels."

Quinn clenched his jaw and struck a closed fist across Dibner's cheek. The older man's head snapped back. This time when he looked up at Quinn, he spat blood.

"Try again," Quinn demanded. "This time, with at least some truth."

"More money," he whispered.

Quinn rubbed his swelling knuckles. He shrugged his shoulders as if thinking about delivering a second blow, but instead turned to Tyler. "He can't even tell the truth when his life depends on it." Setting his sights back on Dibner, he continued. "Fine Frank, I'll explain for you. The reason you left oil and redirected your assets into nuclear is because you tapped the well, didn't you? You saw the writing on the wall. It's the reason there hasn't been a large-scale build on a massive oil refinery within the United States since 1973. Why is that Frank?"

Silence followed the rain plinking against the roof of Tyler's utility van.

"The real reason," Quinn said, "is because you knew then, those many years ago, that there was an end to oil, that there's only so much to use before we run out. They knew in the 70s but couldn't reveal it then. They'd have lost their precious money.

"People would've already made the shift. Solar, wind, and even nuclear would've gotten a better billing. But they kept the lie alive. And it percolated for years. They controlled it at the congressional level. They have their hands in everybody's pockets. Big oil, just like big tobacco, proved once again that they could control politics, because in the end, money is the root of all power. And they have the lion's share." Quinn's boots sunk deeper into the mud as the rain continued its assault. But none of it distracted his focus from his captive audience. "Our buddy Dibner here, well, he saw the writing on the wall. But instead of coming clean, he took another path and put his dirty money into nuclear. And that's what brought you here to Oregon, isn't it? Lucky for me, you came a couple days early."

Dibner's shoulders slumped and his chin rested on his chest. "What are you going to do with me?"

"I'm going to make sure that the punishment fits the crime, and, as the leader of a group who looks out for the world when others can't, I deem you one of the worst offenders. And for that, the punishment is death."

Dibner's eyes widened. Rainwater streamed down Dibner's face, joining the tears freely falling. Frank Dibner stared straight into Tyler Pierce's eyes. His silent demand reached outward, pleading for mercy.

Tyler's stomach sank with regret. He felt the bile rise and fought back against the urge to vomit. Conflict drilled holes in his gut. But in the end,

Tyler knew there was nothing he could do. He was afraid of Quinn. Deathly afraid.

Quinn had racked up a number of assault charges over the course of his thirty-odd years of life and had even done a stint in prison for assaulting several police officers at a protest years back.

But murder? Tyler had never thought Quinn would do that. As the only witness capable of stopping him, Tyler stood idly by. And for a brief moment, he welcomed the heavy downpour, which offered a reprieve from Dibner's whimpering.

"He's not going to help you, Frank," Quinn said. "No one can. You had a chance to help the world years ago, and you didn't. You pawned it off to my generation. Well, guess what? This is how I'm taking it back. But don't worry, you won't be alone for long. Hell's going to need a bigger waiting room." Quinn took a step back and surveyed the marshy landscape as if it were his kingdom. "There's room for dozens, shit, hundreds of graves out here."

Quinn cut the bindings holding Dibner to the chair. His wrists and ankles were still bound by a rope encased in duct tape. He looked like a prisoner on a chain as he tried to shove himself free of the chair. A desperate move by a desperate man. But Dibner's physical prowess did not support the commitment shown in his eyes. For all his flailing, he did little more than wriggle the chair deeper into the mud. With one swift kick, Quinn knocked Dibner out of the chair. The oil tycoon was face down in the mud when Quinn grabbed him by his hair, dragging him into the hole. Dibner rolled to his back, his face and body plastered with clumps of brown muck. Using his legs as momentum, Dibner forced himself into a seated position within his grave. He frantically clawed at the slick mud wall. All of his efforts ceased when Quinn pressed a gun to his head.

"Where'd you get that?" Tyler stepped back, and by some unconscious reaction, and one he immediately regretted, he threw his hands up. He was just as surprised as Dibner at the sight of the firearm. It seemed to have materialized out of nowhere.

"Please, I can't die like this!" Dibner cried. "Let me go. What do you want? Money? I've got tons of it. Name your price!"

"You've been able to buy yourself out of every single problem you've ever faced. Makes sense that you would assume you could buy your way out of this one. For once, you can't." He jutted his chin toward Tyler. "Fill it in."

"Please, no!" Dibner twisted, wedging himself deeper into the muddy soup.

Tyler looked at the shovel on the ground, then back at Quinn. Quinn looked down at the gun in his hands, still pointed at Dibner, then made eye contact with Tyler. The implication was clear. Either shovel the dirt, or the gun would turn in his direction.

In the split second of hesitation where he weighed his options, Tyler thought about his brother-in-law, a man he'd known had taken a human life before. One thing was certain. His brother-in-law never would've done it like this. He also thought of his brother-in-law's bravery and how ashamed he'd be of Tyler if he could see him now. But his brother-in-law wasn't around anymore. And Tyler wasn't brave. His only measure of defiance was in the moment's pause and the hard stare he gave Quinn.

Tyler, feeling the weakness of his conviction, bent down and picked up the shovel by its handle and began knocking the heavy dirt into the shallow grave. He looked at the fir trees surrounding the embankment and wondered if anyone would ever find Dibner. And then, more selfishly, he wondered if anyone would ever find something linking Tyler to this grave.

The rain lightened as he continued to shovel the dirt on Dibner. The older man flailed, but the strength of his resolve weakened as the heavy mud weighed down his arms. His writhing only worked to seal him in tighter until he couldn't budge at all. His legs were no longer visible. Dibner stopped moving altogether. Tyler stopped too. He feared, or maybe even hoped, that Dibner had a heart attack. That he didn't have to suffer the terrible fate of being buried alive. Upon closer inspection, Tyler realized Dibner was mumbling quietly. Maybe he was praying. Maybe he was saying goodbye to loved ones. Who knew? What Tyler did know was that Dibner no longer fought and had resigned himself to death.

Quinn looked satisfied with Tyler's work. It was also the first time he seemed to notice the rain and how soaked through he was. Quinn no longer pointed the gun at Dibner's head, instead now holding it loosely at his side. He then squatted low. His gun hand rested over his bent knee. Quinn looked like a gunslinger of the Old West as he spoke to the man in the grave. "Frank, your death might be the greatest contribution you've made in your pathetic life. In time, millions and millions of years from now, maybe your body will become part of the crude oil that lined your pockets."

Tyler contemplated how flawed Quinn's logic was. During his short time at Fairhaven Community College, he'd learned the great debate over dinosaur fossils becoming crude oil had been dispelled. It was billions of years of carbon-based plankton that had created the oil reserves. At least that's what his teacher had said. But he was in no position to correct Quinn's logic, especially when the man he considered arguing with held a gun.

Quinn continued his rant. "And if the critters find you, they'll eat you or you'll decompose and go back into the soil. Maybe a tree will grow where you once were and contribute to the oxygen supply. But really, your death doesn't even begin to satisfy the indifference you've shown the world."

Dibner looked like a man in the middle of the ocean, about to give up. His face poked out of the dirt. "Please. I can make it right."

"You've had your chance. Maybe the death of you and your associates will wake the world to the truth."

Tyler worked hard to avoid the man's face with each shovel full, feeling a desperate need to preserve his life for as long as he could. As Dibner's arms and shoulders became packed in earth, Dibner worked his face up higher as dirt continued to rain down on him, covering his flesh in the muddy brown goop.

Tyler didn't know how he'd reconcile his actions tonight, but he knew if he didn't follow through, he would be digging his own grave next to this one.

"Finish up," Quinn ordered. "Don't leave until it's done. And by done, I mean, he's not moving. At all."

With that, the last bit of dirt shrouded Dibner's face and sealed the man in the ground at Quinn's feet. Quinn returned the gun to the small of his back and walked to his Jeep Grand Cherokee. He looked back at Tyler before continuing on. "We'll meet up tomorrow to discuss our next step."

Next step? Tyler thought. What was he talking about?

They were supposed to get together two days from now to protest the ribbon-cutting ceremony for the nuclear alternative authorization at the old Trojan Nuclear site. What the hell was happening? He couldn't imagine Max had known what Quinn's plans had been. But with Quinn out of control, he didn't know what to think.

"Don't look so worried." Quinn lingered after opening the driver's side door. "This is the beginning of a new era for us." He got into his Jeep and drove off, not turning his headlights on until he reached the dirt road toward Fairhaven.

With every shovel load of dirt he'd tossed on Dibner, Tyler felt as though he was burying a part of his soul in the ground with the dying man.

He finished up, tamping the dirt down to make it as flat and even as possible. Tyler scattered pine needles over the top, doing his best to make it look undisturbed.

Then he walked away.

The wind whistled as it swept through the Douglas fir pines around him, calling forward the memory of Dibner's haunting whimper. Tyler stood at the back of his van. Both doors were open but did little to deflect the wind. He set the mud-covered shovel in the back amongst the PVC pipe and other odds and ends his sister kept stashed in the van for her construction projects at her new diner.

He sat in the van. The heat from the vents working to lift the thaw from his bones. He looked out the side mirror. And then in the back of the van. He had an idea, one that might be enough to save his conscience, if not his soul.

# TWO

Hatch rode shotgun in Cruise's Jeep. The late-morning light streaked Cruise's hair in glowing bits of orange and gold as they drove through the security checkpoint at the Naval Amphibious Base Coronado. They passed the chow hall on the left where Hatch saw groups of young men in wet, sandy uniforms, hoisting rigid inflatable boats on top of their heads and moving in a stilted procession away from the mess hall.

"They look exhausted." Hatch noted the vacant stares in the passing men, their eyes locked on the person right in front of them or on the ground at their shuffling boots.

"It's Hell Week," Cruise said. "Day two for this group. Food is a necessity to survive the week, and it's a mile and a half from the SEAL training base to the chow hall on the NAB side. That's a nine-mile minimum just to get their three square meals a day, and the boats don't make that shuffle any easier."

"Tough training," Hatch said.

"You've been through the School of Hard Knocks, too."

"Yeah, but the water adds a different element. Not sure I could make it through that."

Cruise gazed at the gaunt faces of the men passing by, pausing as if seeing himself in their image. "To become a killer of killers, one must go through a metamorphosis. And those students are in the chrysalis phase. When they emerge from the other side of this week, they'll be so much more than they ever imagined they could be. A true rebirth of mind and body."

Hatch remembered the gauntlet she had run, and the forging it had taken to harden her body, mind, and soul. Those lessons began with her father as a child and continued to this day. She also recalled the price she'd paid to become the person she was. Her body had become a hardened exterior marred with marks of war, like that of a Spartan's shield. Hatch ran her hand along the scar traversing her forearm, the physical reminder of the path she'd traveled since the moment her life changed forever. Her personal fork in the road etched in her twisted flesh.

They pulled up to a parking spot outside the pool area. In the distance, off to the right, the bay appeared as calm as the chemically treated water in front of them. Hatch exited the Jeep and spotted Ed Banyan—the newest member of Talon—standing at the gate with a broad smile plastered on his face. He'd been with the team the last couple of months, and was quickly becoming one of Hatch's favorite people.

Banyan was a man whose military combat experience rivaled Hatch's own. He always managed a smile, never seeming affected by his past traumas. A family man with a level head, it took quite a bit of pressure from Cruise to get Banyan to finally concede and join the ranks of Talon Executive Services. The two men had a bond rooted in surviving Hell Week together. That painful and sleepless week forged an unbreakable friendship. Hatch thought of the SEAL trainees back at the chow hall and the new generation of warriors being forged into brotherhood.

Hatch and Cruise had both received a text message earlier this morning from Banyan. He was eager to show them something but unwilling to spoil any element of surprise.

"Well, let's see what Banyan's all hyped up about." Cruise exited and slammed the driver-side door to his Jeep. Throwing his friend a wave, he and Hatch made their way toward the outdoor pool's open gate.

The pool was Olympic-sized. Fifty meters in length, twenty-five meters across, and a twenty-meter deep end, tapering off into a shallow four-foot depth on the opposite side.

"I hope you guys brought your swimsuits," Banyan said.

Hatch snapped the shoulder strap of her suit hidden beneath her clothes. "As instructed."

"Still not sure why you called us here," Cruise said. "Thought today was a range day."

"We can go to the range after. Everybody knows we can all shoot."

Hatch met the man's smile. "I can give my trigger finger a rest today."

In the months since leaving Jericho Falls and seeing Dalton Savage, Hatch had buried her head in the sand, unable to decipher the meaning behind Savage's stolen kiss, or what her kissing him back meant for her and Cruise. So far, she'd decided to do what she did best—avoid the matter altogether, and pour her energy into training. The newly formed, albeit smaller, team now consisted of Cruise, Banyan, and Hatch, with Jordan Tracy at the helm. Aside from consuming most of her time, the constant training served as a necessary distraction to her constant raging inner conflict.

Days turned into weeks, which turned into months without having contacted Savage. That meant months spent in a paralyzed emotional state, making it impossible to commit fully to Cruise. She knew he could feel her pulling away from him, and she sensed a talk coming. She'd dismissed it several times in the previous months, cutting it off at the pass before he uttered the words. But how long could she keep them both in limbo?

On the battlefield, decisions came to her as naturally as breathing, the automatic response built within her neural network. But when it came to navigating her heart, she stood frozen on the edge of a minefield. And she could only stay in stasis for so long before she'd have to move forward. Hatch was stuck in her past, and the passing of time wasn't helping to heal her.

"I have something really exciting to show you." Banyan beamed, his bright energy removing Hatch from her all-too familiar inner monologue.

From behind his back, Banyan pulled out what looked like a child's toy steering wheel. It was gaudy and bright yellow, and had two hand grips, one of which Banyan used to hold on to the device. It had a small display system that looked like the navigation screen in a car. The front end protruded out into a convex, rounded end like the nose of an airplane. Connected along the bottom were four small fans, each about three inches in diameter.

"Guys, meet the Swim Buddy." Banyan looked like a child with his favorite toy on Christmas morning.

"I thought I was your swim buddy," Cruise said.

Banyan laughed. "This thing right here is going to revolutionize tactical water insertion." He gestured at Hatch with the device. "How long can you hold your breath?"

"I would say a minute thirty, maybe a minute forty-five."

"Pretty good," Banyan said. "Definitely above average."

Hatch shrugged. "Running helps, I guess." She didn't have an extensive level of experience in water-born operations. As far as Hatch was concerned, she was an earth pig, a term her father had affectionately used when referring to the land warrior.

"I'd like to test this with you, see if we can get you above the two-minute mark, and see what my little yellow buddy here can do. I believe experience is the best teacher."

"I'd second that."

"How comfortable are you in the water?"

Hatch thought of the trainees she'd seen on the drive in. The various states of shock were likely in part due to the extreme water evolutions endured during training. Hatch had been privy to the experience through Cruise's colorful retelling of his own personal experiences.

"Probably not as much as you guys."

"Well, let me give you a baseline. At BUD/s, SEAL trainees are tested through several evolutions. One of those tests is a water confidence drill in which they are required to complete a fifty-meter underwater swim."

Hatch eyed the pool, calculating the distance. She wondered how an earth pig would fare. Hatch had a feeling she would soon have that answer.

Banyan had an air of nostalgia in his voice as he continued. "We used the deep end here in this very pool. Its twenty-meter depth is used for other challenges like underwater knot tying among other things, like the beehive. Nothing like putting a hundred plus bodies into the middle of a pool and treading with your hands above the water. It creates a chaotic churn."

Cruise chuckled. "And ten minutes later, you're fighting for your life."

"Sounds terrible." Hatch imagined the burning in her arms, legs, and lungs.

"It can be," Cruise said.

"All of it *can* be," Banyan said. "Unless you've got the right mindset. Let's get you acclimated to the water. I'm going to have you do the fifty-meter underwater confidence swim, the way we do it in SEAL training. When you step off the side of the deck, you cannot dive or pencil drop into the water. You need to scissor kick and slow your momentum. We don't want anybody cheating the process. Once you're in, keep yourself beneath the surface of the water and complete a forward somersault, all the while remaining underwater. After completing the roll, begin your swim. Progress forward twenty-five meters to the other side of the wall. Touch the wall with both hands before turning and making your return the twenty-five meters across. Do not come up for air until you've touched this other side."

Hatch felt as though Banyan spoke to her the way he would if delivering this message to a group of SEAL trainees, where he'd spent the last two years of his time in the service.

She took a couple of deep breaths, trying to build up an oxygen reserve. Hatch also knew that by taking in the deep, controlled breath, she was calming her mind and body. This practice had served her well in the past and was helping now.

Banyan leaned in and spoke less like an instructor and more like a friend. "It really helps if you make your way to the bottom of the pool before trying to go across. The pressure from the water above will help minimize the amount of oxygen depletion by your muscles. The deeper you go, the easier it is. And don't forget to Valsalva your ears. Even at twenty meters, the pressure can be intense for those who don't know how to relieve it. Just manipulate your jaw, the way you would if you were trying to pop your ears during a plane's descent."

Hatch took in all the instructions given to her by Banyan, memorizing them in steps.

"I'm not timing you. There's no clock to beat. Remember, this is just an underwater confidence evolution."

Hatch nodded and took a moment to disrobe. The twisted scar covering her right arm left her feeling exposed as the morning's sunlight warmed the puffy tapestry of that fateful day. She took one last deep breath, exhaling as much of the air out of her lungs as she could before inhaling once more. A split second later, her body launched upward, leaving the warmth of the concrete deck, exchanging it for the cold water. Submerging beneath the surface, she scissor-kicked her feet to keep from going too deep. Hatch then folded her body forward and performed a single rotation somersault, forcing some of her precious air through her nostrils to block the water from entering, then swam hard with her arms, pulling herself down toward the bottom of the pool. Standing on the outside of the pool looking down, the twenty meters depth didn't seem that bad. But now as she struggled to her target, it felt twice as deep.

The light dimmed as she descended. Her stomach skimmed across the smooth bottom. She pulled and long stroked with her arms down by her sides, alternating and then kicking like a frog with her feet.

*Pull, glide, kick. Pull, glide, kick.*

Her fingers touched the wall on the far side. The halfway point. Twenty-five meters completed. She felt a tingling in her arms that stretched to her lungs, where it burned like molten lava. She kicked hard against the wall, trying to use the force to guide her forward and minimize the energy she had to expend. At this point, every movement she made burned critical oxygen.

*Pull, glide, kick.*

Her shoulders were on fire. The lack of air threatened to cramp her quadriceps. Bubbles escaped her mouth as she let out an involuntary whimper. Instinct caused her to attempt to rebreathe the air she exhaled. Water flooded her mouth and throat. She coughed, expelling the last bit of oxygen in her lungs.

Her body screamed. Her brain screamed. She wanted to scream.

Hatch felt a type of desperation she'd never felt before, and for a moment, panic set in. She thought of Cruise and Banyan looking down from above. With ten meters to go, the wall ahead blurred. Her body felt detached and would no longer cooperate with her mind. Without control, she was like a boat without a motor. Unable to maintain her depth, Hatch's natural buoyancy lifted her body upward. She ascended toward the surface. Hatch made a last-ditch effort and pulled as hard as she could. Out of oxygen, tunnel vision setting in, she drifted forward.

# THREE

*We are gathered here today—It sounded as though he were composing a eulogy, and a terrible one at that.* Yohei Suzuki crossed out the line he'd just written with his silky black ballpoint pen. The paper taunted him as he rolled the instrument between his fingers. His father would've disapproved of using such an instrument to craft this speech. His father had been a principled man, both in business and in life. Suzuki sought his approval even after death. He heard his father's words as though he were standing right behind him. A pen or pencil doesn't give pause to the fevered mind. His father always wrote using a quill and inkwell. He'd said it forced the user to take a moment to craft the words in his mind before setting them to paper.

Suzuki felt his father's disappointment as he stared down at his hasty attempt at formulating the words for a speech he wasn't prepared to give. Grunting, he tore the sheet from the legal pad, crumpling it in frustration and dropping it to his feet where six other failed attempts lay in waste.

Ice rattled in his water glass as a slight bout of turbulence shook the private jet, and Suzuki checked his seatbelt to make sure it would keep him in his chair in case of an emergency. A moment later, the speaker crackled to life.

"Sorry about the bumps. We just hit a pocket of turbulence. Should be a smoother flight from here on out."

A hiss of static punctuated the end of the pilot's message. Suzuki went back to his legal pad, seeing the ghostlike indentations mocking him. Before he could set pen to paper again, a yawn sounded from across the aisle from where he worked. There sat his eleven-year-old daughter, Akira, and several of her favorite stuffed animals, blankets, and pillows.

The side of her face was cast in the glow of whatever show she'd been watching, now paused. Books and notepads were scattered all around her, but she was looking at her father with a smile on her face, displaying the innocence of a child. However, her eyes glowed with a wisdom beyond her years.

He leaned across the narrow aisle. "Was it my crumpling of the paper or my grunting that brought you out of whatever spell that tablet has you under?"

"I think maybe a little bit of both," she said with a giggle.

He twirled the pen around his middle finger. "I hate writing these things. Speaking engagements were never really my thing."

"I thought Mr. Dibner was giving the speech?"

"Yes, he was supposed to, but I haven't heard from him, so I have to be prepared to go in his place." He rubbed his eyes and thought of his wife. "Your mom always—"

Akira's tablet went dark and she turned toward him with those sad, knowing eyes. She didn't speak, but the expression on her face would've filled pages of the legal pad in front of him. Akira carried the strength and wisdom of her mother. And since his wife's passing, his daughter seemed to be the one carrying much of his burden, too. More than any child should carry.

"Any advice?" Suzuki tapped his pen against the legal pad and scratched his head. "Because I sound like I'm writing something befitting a funeral."

"Well, you need to start with a blank page."

Suzuki held up the fresh sheet on his legal pad.

"That's not what I mean." Rolling her eyes and sighing loudly. "When Ms. Hatterly tells me, I must get a clean page before writing, she's talking about my mind. She says only with a clear mind can you find the truth in your words."

"Well, my mind is blank too, if that helps."

"She says that once your mind has been emptied of all the problems of the day, the worries for tomorrow, and the memories of the past, then and only then can you focus on the here and now."

Suzuki thought of the wisdom in those words and how beneficial they'd be if he could apply them not only to writing this speech, but to his own life. He gave his daughter a gentle smile. "Sounds like the money I pay your teacher is well spent."

Akira's eyes lit up. Adjusting herself in her seat, she slung her legs out and over the edge, toes dangling just above the carpeted flooring.

"What else has she been teaching you?"

"Well, I have a writing assignment of my own I'm working on. It's a poem, a haiku."

"And?" he prodded.

"I haven't been able to clear my mind either."

"That's something we both need to work on. When your mind *is* clear, what's next?"

"Mrs. Hatterly says to speak from the heart." Reaching out of her pod, she placed her hand on his chest.

Suzuki leaned back in his seat. Her gentle touch gave him a sense of renewed energy. "Your mother was always better at this stuff. She would've helped us both."

Just then, Theo Clay approached from the compartment at the front of the plane. He had been seated in the small conference room with Parker Chase, Clay's personal security guard, and a man he never traveled anywhere without. Akira sighed her annoyance at the interruption. "Any luck reaching Frank?" Suzuki asked.

"No. I spoke to his assistant. They're unable to reach him on any of his phones, even his private line." Clay threw his hands up and shrugged. "I guess we'll have to press forward without him."

"It's supposed to be him up on that stage later."

"I'm sure you'll do fine. I'll open for you. Do most of the talking. All you've got to do is give a couple closing remarks about the future of energy and how Aurora Nuclear is going to take the world by storm. Isn't that right, kiddo?"

Theo Clay reached his hand into the pod and gently mussed the girl's hair. Akira pulled back slightly and rolled her eyes, making a "hm" sound.

"Still not on board?" Clay bent down to look Akira in the eyes. "Nuclear power is the future, my dear. Twenty years from now, you'll be thanking me for brokering this deal and getting your father on board."

"There are other alternatives, better ones." Spitting out the words. Clay disengaged from the girl and turned his back to her, shooting a thumb in her direction. "When you're writing your speech, all you really need to do is think of her as your audience. If you can convince her, you can convince the world. I think I'm going to catch a catnap before we land. Tomorrow will be a big day."

Suzuki gave him a terse nod. Clay turned and made his way back to the compartment at the front of the plane.

"Back to the drawing board," Akira said, holding up her poetry notebook. Retreating into her pod, she closed its door and sealed herself from distraction.

Suzuki looked down at the blank pad. Closing his eyes, he took a deep breath, clearing his mind. With the pen in hand, and now armed with the advice offered by his daughter, he began to write, this time from the heart.

# FOUR

A FLICKER OF DARKNESS FORCED HER INNER RESOLVE. ALL THE FEAR, PANIC, and doubts subsided the moment Hatch's fingertips collided with the wall. She clawed at the concrete, assisting her ascension with whatever strength she had left. After surfacing, she grabbed hold of the edge of the pool and lay her face flat on the ground. Deep inhales led to a coughing fit until her lungs were clear.

She felt hands on her arms as Banyan and Cruise attempted to pull her out. Like a wet eel, she slipped from their grasp and pressed down on the edge of the pool deck. If she couldn't get out of the pool under her own power, she'd rather slip back underwater and drown.

After catching her breath, Hatch eyed both men, and with a weak smile, said, "I can see why it's part of the water confidence course. It sure crushed mine."

"You did it!" Banyan looked down at her like she was one of his daughters. "There are plenty who don't. Many who wash out of BUDs here." He crouched down and his face drew tight. "But the real question is, after fifty meters underwater, think you'd be able to fight right now?"

Hatch took another breath, inhaling the salty air permeating the base and its surroundings. "I never back down from a fight. But if I'm being honest, I'd probably need a minute."

He lifted an eyebrow high into his forehead and beamed a smile. "That's where the Swim Buddy comes in."

Cruise was already in his swim trunks with a pair of goggles on.

Banyan continued. "The distance would improve exponentially with an oxygen tank, like a Draeger rebreather. The Swim Buddy doesn't have any oxygen built into it, not yet at least, but it uses the same low-bubble technology so you won't see a stream of bubbles rising to the surface when it's deployed below the ten-foot mark. I'm gonna have Cruise run it through a quick test while you catch your breath."

"If you don't mind, I'd like to give it a try." Hatch felt the need to test herself again and beat the panic that had surfaced back down to the depths of wherever it came from.

"Sure thing. I'm not going to argue with that look of determination you've got plastered on your face." Banyan handed the Swim Buddy to Hatch.

"It's a touchscreen, uses a basic navigation system, and also has the option of being put into manual operation."

Hatch held the device in her hands, gripping it along the handles on each side. It was surprisingly light. Banyan reached over Hatch's shoulder and manipulated the touchscreen, pressing a button that said Manual Operation. He then explained how to use the buttons on the handles to move forward and adjust course. Satisfied with the basics, Hatch handed it back and hopped into the water, the same water that only minutes before had tried to swallow her whole.

"Use the lane marker as your guide. Start at the shallow end, work your way to the deep, back and forth until you need to come up for air." Banyan gave the Swim Buddy the look of a parent sending their child off to school for the first time. "Be careful. She's a one-of-a-kind."

"So am I." Hatch winked and took the contraption into the water with her.

Hatch took two deep breaths, holding the second as she submerged herself under the water and pressed both buttons. The fans propelled her forward while pulling slightly at her arms. Hatch elongated her body, allowing the device to do the brunt of the work. Every once in a while, she provided a gentle dolphin kick.

She kept the nose of the Swim Buddy pointing downward and skimmed the bottom of the pool as instructed. She was shocked at how soon she reached the fifty-meter mark before making the turn and ascending the slope of the pool's bottom, heading back toward the other side where Banyan and Cruise stood watching.

Her lungs began that same familiar sting and tickle she'd experienced earlier as she touched the far wall a third time. The pressure in her lungs was intense, and she let out some air in small bursts. She endured the feeling of oxygen deprivation for as long as possible until she had managed four laps, covering a total distance of two hundred meters.

"Minute forty-two," Cruise called out.

"Pretty damn good," Banyan said. "Especially after stressing your lungs the way you did on the first swim. Two hundred meters in a minute forty-two, that's fast."

"That's really fast." Cruise hopped into the water. "My turn."

The water obscured the scars on his legs from the damage he'd received in Alaska as he waded over to Hatch and took the Swim Buddy. She glanced over his torso, which appeared untouched by age, and if anything, had gotten trimmer with time. He had made a full recovery, and in Hatch's opinion, was in better shape now than before the incident in Alaska. But that was Cruise. Once challenged, he would always push himself to the next level.

"Have a good swim." Hatch pulled herself back out of the water and moved alongside Banyan.

"And go." Banyan set his stopwatch.

Cruise submerged and headed off across the pool floor toward the deep end.

"That's an amazing tool you've created," Hatch said.

"Thanks."

"Where'd you come up with the name Swim Buddy?"

"You have it in the Army, right? Battle buddy?"

Hatch nodded.

"In SEAL training, you're assigned a swim buddy. The selection course requires you to swim five hundred meters using either breaststroke or sidestroke. To even be considered for SEAL training, applicants need to swim it in under twelve minutes and thirty seconds. But candidates shoot for eight minutes and thirty seconds to be considered competitive. Swimmers are then paired by their abilities. One prerequisite to moving on to each phase in training is each trainee must complete a two-mile ocean swim under certain time parameters, with each phase of training requiring a faster time than its predecessor. A swim buddy is what we call the matched pair of swimmers. They're basically tethered and are told to stay together for the duration of those two-mile swims. A way to keep each other safe in the open ocean. Cruise was my swim buddy, and I can honestly say there is no one better."

Cruise came up, touched the wall near their feet, pushed off and returned the other way. His movements looked effortless, as if he were part dolphin. The reflection of the sunlight blinded them to his movements as he propelled himself toward the middle of the pool.

"He saved my life out there." Banyan looked away from the bay side and out to where the ocean lay just beyond view.

"How so?" Hatch asked.

"That's for another time."

Hatch nodded, accepting Banyan's dismissal and making a mental note to inquire later. Banyan looked at his stopwatch. Cruise was at three minutes and nearing the far side of the pool. "How many laps has he done?"

"If he gets back here again before coming up, five hundred meters."

Hatch watched the water, bouncing her eyes between the stopwatch and Cruise when she caught sight of Jordan Tracy, commander of their unit at Talon Executive Services. He walked down the ramp and onto the pool deck, keeping step with Cruise, who was still underwater and moving along at a steady clip. Cruise touched the side. He released the last bit of air as he broke through the shimmering surface of the pool.

"Three minutes, thirty seconds," Banyan called out.

"Thought you guys were going to the range today," Tracy said, taking a bite of a green apple. A bit of juice escaped his mouth and trickled down the side of his chin. "But then I got your voicemail about trying out some new technology. Figured I'd swing by and make sure you didn't blow the place up."

Cruise held up the Swim Buddy and toggled the propeller off. "Damn fine piece of machinery you got here. Not sure about the banana yellow, though."

"There's one more feature I wanted to show you." Banyan reached down for the device. Cruise hoisted himself out of the water and took a seat on the deck with his legs dangling in the water.

Banyan switched to an autopilot mode and then pressed the "Tether" function. He tossed the Swim Buddy out into the middle of the pool, and they watched as it dropped below the surface and began a wide circle in the middle of the pool.

"The tether function allows the operator to use the Swim Buddy to get to shore, enabling them to carry out the mission topside. Once activated, it will maintain a ten-meter radius circle beneath the surface until it's called back to its locator."

Banyan pressed a button on a handheld device that looked like a watch, and the Swim Buddy halted and then moved underneath the water until it reached the wall at Banyan's feet.

"That's got some serious op potential." Cruise toweled himself off.

Banyan nodded. "Add an oxygen tank or a rebreather component to this, and you can really extend the distance you can travel with this thing."

"Three and a half minutes?" Hatch said.

Cruise smiled.

"He didn't tell you?" Banyan said. "He's part fish."

Banyan turned to Cruise. "I have a Draeger in the trunk of my Subaru. We could take it to the bay and see what this baby can do."

"Sorry to break up the party," Tracy interrupted. "A contract just came in, and we're up to bat. Get outta those wet clothes. Briefing in an hour."

Cruise glanced at the Swim Buddy in the pool and then gave Banyan a playful slap on the back. "Looks like we'll have to save that test for another day."

# FIVE

Tracy had notified the team to meet at the airfield where they'd boarded the private jet provided by Talon. Once airborne, they gathered for an en route briefing. Cruise and Hatch shared a booth seat. Banyan sat across the table, sharing his seat with his Swim Buddy. The bright yellow nose peeked out just above the tabletop.

Tracy sat across the aisle. A flatscreen monitor arose from a containment unit.

"Sorry to do the briefing on the fly, but the principal is a high-value customer, and we aim to please. The bread and butter of Talon is private security ops. Our team was personally requested. Thanks to Cruise." All eyes shifted in Cruise's direction as Tracy continued. "You might remember about a year ago, you handled an escort for a Yohei Suzuki?"

Cruise nodded. "The Japanese billionaire."

"One and the same. He's kicking off a massive new energy project with his newest company, Aurora Nuclear. He's flying in from Tokyo as we speak for events taking place tomorrow to launch the company."

"Don't billionaires like Suzuki have their own private security team assigned to them?" Hatch asked.

"They'll have one security specialist, Parker Chase, a former Ranger turned security contractor who works for Theo Clay. Clay is Suzuki's right-hand man. But Suzuki himself is standoffish from the use of such services. He thinks it sends the wrong message, but in this case, he's willing to make an exception."

"Better to send the wrong message than get taken for your billions," Banyan added. "Or worse."

"So if he doesn't normally hire security," Hatch said. "Why the change?"

"A couple factors," Tracy said. "Suzuki's business partner, Frank Dibner, has been unreachable."

"Does Suzuki suspect foul play?" Cruise asked.

"Nothing to point in that direction. But Dibner's absence so close to the launch of Aurora Nuclear is definitely a cause for concern. Especially since Dibner is one of the company's senior-most board members and slated to give the presentation speech."

Hatch and Cruise exchanged a look.

"I know what you're thinking," Tracy said. "We're not here for Dibner. This isn't an investigation. This is a by-the-book protection detail. That means we are here to protect the asset, Suzuki. If there's something criminal afoot, then the authorities will handle it. Right now, all we know is that Dibner was in town a day or two early and hasn't been seen in the last eighteen hours."

"That's one of the factors," Hatch said. "What's the other?"

"Suzuki is traveling with his eleven-year-old daughter, Akira. He's concerned about her safety. In light of some recent protests, his concerns are valid. Several activist groups have their sights set on Aurora Nuclear. Bringing nuclear energy back to Oregon has people up in arms. Suzuki worries there could be some unforeseen dangers."

"Why not just leave his daughter at home?" Banyan asked.

"She has been traveling with him ever since his wife died several years back," Cruise said.

"Here are photographs of both of them." Tracy pressed a button on his tablet, and the monitor came to life with the images of Suzuki and his daughter. "Cruise, anything that you can add from your past experience with Suzuki?"

"He's professional. Very discreet. Being invisible is a must. We're gonna have to blend in."

"What are we doing about weapons?" Hatch asked.,

"The Glock 23 should be sufficient, concealable in business attire, and the mag capacity can handle most close-in threats. Anybody have a problem with that?"

Everyone shook their heads.

"Cruise and Hatch will be the on-site physical security. Banyan and I will provide overwatch. Banyan, I know you've got plenty of experience in the teams, but I want you to sit back on the control side and observe how the team operates."

Banyan looked a little hurt by the news.

"Don't worry," Cruise said. "You've got your Swim Buddy to keep you company."

Banyan extended his middle finger and winked.

"All right, let's run through the schedule and plan of events. We'll land in Portland, get to the hotel, and have a little downtime before we meet with Suzuki. The major events will take place tomorrow, starting in the morning.

"We'll provide escort and security to the first location, the former home of the Trojan Nuclear Power Plant in Columbia County, about twelve miles north of Mount Saint Helens. It's a decommissioned nuclear site, but Dibner thought it would be a great location to reinvigorate the nuclear power initiative they've conceptualized.

"There's going to be a brief ceremony in which remarks will be made, followed by a small catered reception. There have been rumblings from several of the local activist groups about Aurora Nuclear's initiative, and we are expecting there to be a strong contingent of protestors standing in defiance. Our tech team is doing its job to isolate and identify any potential threats among the activists, and local law enforcement is providing an area off-site for demonstrators to protest that will keep them from the actual ceremony. This will hopefully lower our threat potential, but we have to be prepared. If there are extremists among the protestors, they may slip through the cracks, so be vigilant.

"Total time at the ceremony for Suzuki is about one hour, after which time we will escort him by car to the town of Fair Haven in Tillamook County, several hours south. Banyan and I will remain shoreside to facilitate any needs that arise. Cruise and Hatch will take a helicopter to the offshore location of the nuclear transfer station under construction. You'll be there in time for a small gathering of people that will be ferried over for an evening ribbon cutting. After the ceremony, you will accompany Suzuki and his daughter as they return to Fair Haven. We will then escort them to Portland, and they will fly back to Tokyo that night.

"It's a one-day op with a lot of moving parts and a lot of potential choke points, so use this time while we're in the air to go over map routes, find alternatives, identify threats, and come up with your working plan so we have a point-by-point itinerary that we can brief Suzuki on when we see him. All the information I have is in your tablets. Use the time wisely."

With that, Tracy dropped the screen back into the lacquered display case, and he moved off to the cockpit.

"He said we'd have a few hours of lag time before we meet with Suzuki, right?" Hatch asked.

"Yeah, why?" Cruise said.

"Ever feel like the forces of nature are pushing you?"

"How do you mean?"

"Graham Benson." She rubbed the scar on her right arm, avoiding Cruise's stare. Hatch blamed herself for the hesitation that cost him his life. "His wife and daughter live in Fairhaven. I'm thinking about talking to his wife Shyla. Thinking about telling her everything about that day."

"It might be the closure you've been looking for. It might allow you to move forward." His voice dropped into a whisper. "So that we can move forward."

Maybe there was some truth in that. And maybe she *could* move forward. Hatch decided in that moment that it would be worth finding out.

# SIX

Theo Clay turned his tablet's screen toward Suzuki. He was closer than Suzuki would have preferred, but the limousine's interior was smaller than he was used to. The limo had been late picking them up from the tarmac. Clay had admonished the driver, a little too harshly for Suzuki's taste, but punctuality was essential in the business world. It was one of the things Suzuki liked most about his colleague.

Clay was a close talker by nature, anyway, always pressing the boundaries of Suzuki's personal bubble. He was close enough that Suzuki could make out the hint of whiskey on the man's breath.

"Sir, I want to run through the itinerary for tomorrow one more time just so you have it. Our press conference will be held at ten o'clock in the morning at the decommissioned Trojan Nuclear site. After your speech, there will be a short meet-and-greet with select members of the media. We've arranged to have a caterer provide refreshments for the attendees."

"I did not agree to a *meet-and-greet*."

"Frank did," Clay said.

"Any luck finding him?"

"No."

"Take the meet-and-greet off the schedule."

"Sir, I can't do that. We've got local congressmen coming. Some of our biggest investors will be there. It's an opportunity to press the flesh and build some momentum behind this thing. The support is vital. We don't want to repeat Trojan Nuclear. Why do you think tomorrow's ceremony is so important? Your speech, this program, it's the future of nuclear power. And the activism is just as extreme now, if not more so than it was then. So, I'm sorry, but it's too important to cancel."

"Fine." Suzuki's eyes drifted from the screen to his daughter across from them. Her feet were tucked up, and she was scribbling on her pad. But he knew she was listening. She always listened. Sometimes he felt she could hear his thoughts. She was intuitive in the same way his wife had been, in the way Suzuki himself had never been. Clay interrupted his ruminations with more talking of plans.

"It's a bit of a drive from Trojan Nuclear back to Fairhaven. From there we'll fly from Fairhaven by helicopter to the nuclear transfer station. The guests will arrive soon after by way of boat. After the ribbon cutting, our head engineer will give a tour of the facility, then a black-tie affair on the helicopter pad at sunset to celebrate."

Akira grunted, and Suzuki took notice of his daughter's eyes and her raised brow, as if asking a silent question.

"What am I forgetting?" Suzuki said to his daughter, looking past the tablet in front of him.

"It's my birthday, and you promised me I could decide what I want."

"Of course, my dear. But you haven't told me what it is that you want this year."

"I want you." She beamed. "All to myself."

"And what do you want to do?"

"I want to watch the sunset with you." Her innocence was almost too much.

Suzuki heard Clay sigh to himself, brushing Suzuki with his whiskey-soaked exhale. He narrowed his eyes at Clay. "Do you have a problem with me spending time with my daughter on her birthday?"

"No. But is there a reason why it must take place right in the middle of our reception? Couldn't you take her for ice cream or whatever afterwards?"

The tires of the limo struck a pothole, nearly jostling the tablet from

Clay's hands and causing the pen in Akira's hand to run across the page. She muttered something in frustration. Suzuki didn't know if it was directed at the errant mark on her page, or at him for forgetting her birthday request.

Suzuki nudged Clay's tablet back in the other man's direction, giving a dismissive wave. "I've got the schedule. We've been over it enough. We'll figure out the reception later. Listen Theo, you've been a big help. Everything you've done to get this program where it is now, I couldn't have done it without you. The way you've kept things running after my wife, I..."

Now it was Clay who waved a dismissive hand. "Please, sir. It was my pleasure."

"You should be the one to give the speech tomorrow."

Clay gave a half smile. "But I am. I'm introducing you."

Suzuki used a cane to balance himself as he shimmied his way into the seat next to his daughter. She looked up at him, disappointment in her eyes.

"Hey." Suzuki tapped the breast pocket of his suit. "It worked."

"The speech?" Akira asked.

"I did what your teacher said. After I cleared my mind, I filled the page."

"And?"

"And I wrote from the heart."

"Then it'll be perfect." Akira tapped her pad. "I wish that advice had worked as well for me."

"Let me see what you've got so far." Suzuki looked over his daughter's shoulder as she turned the pad toward him. No words. Just a drawing. A calm, flat ocean with the beautiful sun setting at the horizon. Along the shore were two silhouetted figures and one seagull flying off in the distance.

"I thought you were working on a poem."

"I am. It helps me to draw. I'm trying to write something about the ocean. I just haven't figured it out yet."

"It's a beautiful drawing."

"It was supposed to be you and me, but now it has that big line across it." Akira traced the black line from the dark water where she had been outlining up into the sunrise. "The picture is ruined."

"Not so. My old karate instructor used to tell me a mistake is another opportunity for newfound perfection."

"What does that mean?"

"You can take any tragedy, any circumstance that didn't go your way, and turn it into something positive."

Akira looked down at her drawing, at the line it had made. She bit her bottom lip the way she always did when she was thinking, another trait she'd inherited from her mother. Then she looked at him once more.

"I could turn it into a wave."

Smiling. "You see."

"A really big wave."

"Well, it's a big ocean." Suzuki looked at his daughter as she went back to work on her sketch.

A few minutes later, the limousine came to a stop. The door opened. Parker Chase stood by as two members of the hotel staff approached to greet them. The male popped the limo's trunk to retrieve their luggage.

The second staff member walked with her hands behind her back toward the limo as Suzuki stepped from it and stood beside Theo Clay, who had already gotten out.

Walking past Parker Chase, she brought her hands from behind her back. Holding a cup of a dark, thick liquid, she threw it onto Suzuki. Akira was about to exit the vehicle when her father stepped in the way to protect her.

The dark viscous fluid spread across his silk shirt. The Rorschach blot stretched to his Armani suit. The smell stung his nose. Suzuki recognized it instantly. Motor oil.

Before the girl could drop the cup and run, Parker Chase tackled her to the ground. Securing her in flex cuffs, he hauled her toward hotel security while the other attendant held his hands up, wide-eyed and shocked. More hotel staff rushed out, including several security officers.

The girl yelled back at Suzuki as Chase hauled her away. "This is just the beginning. Mother Nature has an answer for you. Wait until her waves crash down upon you and break you like twigs!"

Chase turned the woman over to security as the hotel manager came out, mortified, and apologized for the actions of his employee. He promised that he'd already fired her and the police would arrest her. The manager himself then assisted the male employee in unloading the suitcases from the trunk.

Suzuki turned to Akira and inspected his daughter. "Are you okay?"

"Yes, I'm fine." Akira nodded, clutching the art pad against her chest.

Turning to Clay, he wiped some of the excess oil from his hands onto his already-ruined suit. "This is why I've added more protection for tomorrow's events."

Clay questioned, "Who did you hire? All security decisions are supposed to be run through me. And besides, we have Parker."

"THE COMPANY I used last year, Talon Executive Services."

"And where are they?"

"They'll arrive later. I told them I didn't need them until tomorrow. Have Parker get them up to speed when they arrive."

"Sir, you were supposed to have dinner tonight with—"

Suzuki held up a finger, cutting him off. "I think there's been enough scheduling for tonight. I plan to take a long, uninterrupted bath. And then I plan to spend time with my daughter. If that's okay?"

Suzuki watched Parker Chase following the security officers escorting the disgruntled staff member before turning his attention back to Clay. "If that had been a gun, I'd already be dead."

## SEVEN

A BEAM OF SUNLIGHT PENETRATED THE CLOUD COVER AS THE RAIN LET UP from a steady pour to a gentle drizzle. A change from the deluge they'd experienced since landing in Portland. Banyan drove. Tracy sat up front, giving the backseat of the SUV to Hatch and Cruise.

"Sounds good. Should you need us sooner, you have my number." Tracy ended the call and shifted in his seat, turning toward the back. "That was Parker Chase. Head of security for Theo Clay, Mr. Suzuki's business partner. He said he'll brief the team tonight at eight."

Hatch looked at the clock. They'd have a couple of hours before meeting with Chase.

"That gives us a couple hours of downtime." Cruise noted.

"I've got something I need to do first." Her expression didn't match Cruise's enthusiasm. Hatch knew she'd been absent as of late, both in mind and body. Sensing the growing strain on their relationship, all from her silent indecisiveness.

"You've got a window of free time, but I wouldn't venture too far. There was an incident at the hotel," Tracy said. "One of the staff members threw a full cup of motor oil on Mr. Suzuki when he arrived."

"Where was Clay's security at the time?" Hatch asked.

"I guess he was able to stop her. She's since been detained."

"Her?" Cruise cocked an eyebrow. "That explains it. Security lowers their guard for females."

Hatch thought about firing off a counterargument to this claim, but she knew Cruise was right. Women, the elderly, and children were often overlooked as threats. A dropping of the guard, Hatch had used this to her advantage on more than one occasion. "Do we know about any additional threats?"

"Nothing yet. She's only been with the hotel a short time, but Chase did some digging and found her Facebook page full of environmental activism rants. At face value, she doesn't appear to be connected. But we want to stay vigilant tomorrow. All it takes is for one of these activists to slip past with something a little more potent than motor oil."

Tracy pulled up to the front of the hotel and the four exited the vehicle.

"We've got an additional SUV here at the hotel," Tracy said. "In the event we need to split up at any point. I've also taken the liberty of ordering us some professional attire. To help us blend in at the conference." He opened the trunk and pulled out four separate covered hangers, one for each of them.

Hatch grabbed hers. "I need to borrow one of the cars."

Tracy threw her the keys. "Get back soon. We've only got a few hours before the meet."

Cruise glanced at his watch before bringing his cobalt blue eyes up to hers. "I can go with you if you want?"

"This is something I've got to do on my own. You understand, right?"

Cruise took the hit in stride. "Are you sure you're up for it?"

"No." It felt good being honest with him. Ever since she'd held back the fact that she'd seen Savage back in Kentucky, Hatch felt like everything she did was a lie. "I don't know if I'll ever be."

"Did you tell her you're in the area?"

"No. I wasn't sure if I'd be able to do it. But now that I'm here, I don't think I'd be able to look myself in the mirror if I didn't."

"You're sure you're ready to do this?" Cruise asked.

"It's one of those now or never things. So, I guess I'm as ready as I'll ever be."

TSUNAMI

With her new clothes folded under her arm and keys in hand, she pressed the key fob. A chirp guided her to the spare vehicle. A moment later, Hatch was pulling out of the lot, putting Cruise in the rearview as she set off toward Fairhaven to confront Graham Benson's widow.

---

AFTER AN HOUR'S DRIVE WEST, Hatch sat in Shyla Benson's driveway, watching the rain splash her windshield. She noticed flickers of light through the front windows, and movement inside. She saw an older woman, Shyla's mother maybe, and a young girl, Shyla's daughter. It looked like they were moving between the kitchen and dining room. Then she spotted Shyla.

Despite what had happened, Hatch had yet to meet with the woman. To let her know what had really happened to her husband. Hatch realized a pattern forming. Holding back from telling the truth to those who mattered. To Cruise. To Shyla. At least she was now about to remedy the situation with one of them—even if it meant casting herself in a worse light.

She would come clean, and that's all that mattered. Hatch was hopeful this evening would relieve the heavy burden she'd been carrying, and ultimately provide some peace for her and for Shyla.

Before giving herself the chance to turn back around, she headed out into the rain, towards the front door. After a second of hesitation, she knocked and stepped back, allowing the precipitation to coat her body. Footsteps shuffled inside. The door opened.

"Oh." Shyla froze before Hatch. Her delicate face was framed by the hairs loose from her bun. Her hazel eyes were lined with dark circles underneath. Taking a step back, she studied Hatch with a furrowed brow, head cocked to the side. "I wasn't expecting *you*."

"I was in the area." Hatch interlaced her fingers and brought her pointers to her lip for a moment. "Do you have time to talk?"

Shyla hesitated and folded her arms. "I thought I would have heard from you sooner." She let the words sink in, as though she already knew why Hatch was here.

"I... I picked up the phone to call you, but... well, it doesn't matter. I'm here now."

Shyla unfolded her arms and stepped aside, holding the door open and avoiding Hatch's eyes. "We're just getting dinner ready."

Hatch realized rainwater droplets were falling to the floor from her clothes and hair.

"Let me find you a towel." Shyla vanished into a hallway on the left.

Hatch stood still, not wanting to drip anywhere else. Shyla returned with a towel.

"Thanks." After drying off and removing her shoes, Hatch stepped further into the house. Shyla excused herself to the kitchen to see if her mother needed help. Hatch noticed a little girl in the dining room, drawing a picture.

Hatch took a seat across from the girl, setting the towel over the cushion as a shield from her drenched clothing. She recognized Graham and Shyla Benson's young daughter from the funeral. Remembering the little girl on that day. How distraught she was over her deceased father, how she leaned into her mother and sobbed their shared sorrow.

Today, the girl held an air of composure, if not acceptance.

"Hi there. My name's Rachel."

The girl looked up from her drawing, her little golden curls bouncing as she pondered the strange woman in front of her, maybe recognizing Hatch from her father's funeral. "I'm Maddie." She looked back down at her drawing.

"It's nice to meet you, Maddie. What are you drawing there?"

Maddie grinned, happy to have the strange woman interested in her artwork. "This is my Uncle Tyler. He's the bestest person I know. He'll come over to see us soon, I just know it."

"I don't know about that, Maddie." Shyla stood at the doorway with her hands on her hips, the faintest sadness shrouding her face. "We love Uncle Tyler, but we don't see him very much, huh?"

"I guess not." Maddie frowned. "Why not, Mom? Can he come over soon?"

Shyla bent down to kiss her daughter on the head. "Go see if your grandmother needs help."

Maddie leaped out of her chair and bounded into the kitchen. Shyla took her daughter's spot at the table.

"You have a brother?" Hatch asked, attempting to stall with awkward small talk as long as she could.

"Yeah, Tyler. He just turned twenty. Good guy, but I'm worried about him right now." Shyla sighed and sat forward, leaning her arms on the table. "But that's not why you're here, Rachel."

Hatch looked in the other woman's pleading eyes, realizing she couldn't stall any longer. "I'm sorry for coming with no notice. I just decided it was time to talk to you." Pausing, she looked down at her hands. "About what really happened to Graham."

Shyla sat still and continued staring at Hatch, her expression unreadable. A slight nod of her head prompted Hatch to go on.

"I'm the reason he's dead."

Shyla gasped for air, leaning back in her chair as if blown back by wind. At that same moment, sirens blared from outside the house.

The television hissed warnings of a tsunami threatening the coast, the town of Fairhaven. The word "TSUNAMI" lined the bottom of the screen, repeating in case anyone who flicked on the television hadn't already heard the sirens.

Hatch heard Maddie screaming from the kitchen as her grandmother tried to calm her. Shyla took one last look at Hatch, eyes wild and desperate, before rushing to her daughter, trying to cover her ears and embrace the girl all in one motion.

Hatch saw this as an opportunity to make a break for it. She'd botched her delivery and now hit the panic button. The siren continued to compete with Maddie's screaming.

In the chaos, Hatch jumped from the table and hightailed it through the front door.

Leaping into the car, she sped back to Portland, not stopping to look back.

# EIGHT

Tyler pulled up to a shed in the middle of nowhere. He'd borrowed his sister's utility van again, this time for Quinn's next phase in whatever plan he'd concocted. Trees surrounded the embankment. Blue horizon covered the distance.

He was back at the place where he'd buried Frank Dibner's body. At least, as far as Quinn knew. Tyler looked around the terrain to see the patch of dirt still packed down the way he'd left it the day before. He still hadn't been able to remove the image of Dibner. The way the man had cried and screamed and pleaded for his life. The scene haunted Tyler.

Hopefully, that would be the end of it. Maybe Quinn had realized how insane it all was. Maybe he'd felt some level of remorse and would make it up to Tyler today.

Somehow.

Regardless, Max would be here this time, Tyler was sure. If he were honest, he only cared about seeing her. She made it worth dealing with Quinn's questionable antics. She was the reason Tyler became involved in the first place. He didn't blame her. He blamed his heart.

Tyler still struggled with what ifs. What if he'd known Quinn would go so far as to kidnap someone? Would he still think sticking around to be near Max was worth that?

He found Max and Quinn waiting beside Quinn's Grand Cherokee. Neither spoke. Maxine had her hands clasped together in front of her, a look of exasperation and fatigue plaguing her delicate features. Quinn's arms were folded across his chest as he stared at the coastline just beyond a row of trees, swept into whatever plan he had in store for them.

In his rush to walk over to them, Tyler slammed the van door louder than he'd meant to. Max gave him a shy smile before looking back down at her feet.

"Took you long enough," Quinn barked. "Clock's ticking. We have serious business to discuss."

"I thought you said this was a meeting of The Watch? Where's everyone else?" Tyler asked, avoiding the leader's aggression.

"This is a special mission. Invite only." Quinn sneered. "You should feel lucky you made the list."

"What's our special mission?" Tyler bit the inside of his cheek, recalling what Quinn's last favor had been.

"I'm so glad you asked. Tomorrow's a big day, and we need to be prepared. Aurora Nuclear's making an announcement. The company's leader, Yohei Suzuki, is speaking at the ribbon cutting in place of Frank Dibner." Tyler froze at the mention of the name. Quinn caught his reaction and smirked. "You did good work yesterday, Tyler. And just like yesterday, we need to make sure everything continues to go smoothly. There's a lot riding on this."

"What is this plan of yours?" Tyler asked.

Quinn reached into the bag at his feet and rummaged his hand around before retrieving two pistols. He handed them out as if he were serving candy to a group of trick-or-treaters. Tyler took the weapon in his hand. The bulky weight felt foreign. His only experience with guns came by way of his brother-in-law, and the last time was years ago. Tyler saw the bulge in the front of Quinn's waistline and figured he'd given himself the best of the bunch.

Max almost dropped hers in disgust. She let it dangle from her pointer finger and thumb as she tried to distance her body as though the gun would fly away if she separated herself enough from it. "What the hell,

Quinn?" She looked up at her brother and raised her voice. "Guns? Are you kidding?"

"Oh, relax." Quinn made a 'calm down' gesture with his hands. "They're just for your protection, in case something goes wrong. Besides, only one of us should have to use it, if at all."

"Then why do we all need them?" Tyler asked. "We've never resorted to this before. Tell us what's going on."

"Yeah, Quinn," Max said. "I'm all for saving the environment, but I thought we were here to make change peacefully."

"Jesus, would you both relax? The guns are for the worst-case scenario." His voice lowered and then he muttered under his breath. "Which might be more likely to happen than not."

"Quinn!" Max pressed the gun back into her brother's hand. When he wouldn't accept it, she shoved the pistol into the bag it came from. Horror and rage distorted her otherwise adorable features into an expression Tyler had never seen before, and never wanted to see again.

Quinn doubled down, giving his sister a shove and taking the gun back out of the bag, slamming it into her stomach. He ran a frustrated hand over his short, blond buzzcut. "This needs to be done right. The guy isn't paying us for mistakes. We do it the way I say, and nobody gets hurt."

Silence fell among the three.

Tyler was the first to speak up. "Someone's *paying* us? Was that also why you kidnapped Dibner and made me—"

"Enough about Dibner. This isn't about Dibner."

"Who's Dibner?" Max asked, shock and desperation playing in her eyes as, for the first time, she seemed to recognize her brother for the psychopath he was. She looked to Tyler for an answer, only for him to avert his eyes.

"The less you know, the better. Didn't I teach you anything?" Quinn shook his head with disgust. "Everything comes at a price. Just take the guns and do what I tell you, or you'll be looking at the other end of this barrel."

Tyler knew the last comment was aimed at him as Quinn made sure his hand came to rest on the butt of the gun protruding from his pants. Tyler lowered his head, avoiding the other man's stare. He wondered how he ever ended up here and why Quinn had to take it this far. Sure, Quinn had fallen off the deep end recently, but it hadn't started out this way. When Tyler joined up with this small band of environmental activists, he never imagined things would go so far.

"This money is the answer we've been looking for. It's going to give us the ability to do what we've always dreamed of and more. Do you know how many waterways we can save? How many lives are at stake?"

"What's the price of a human life?" Tyler asked, the words coming out before he could stop them. "And how do you weigh one against another?"

"Don't talk back to me, Tyler. You're in this just as much as I am. Maybe more. Still got that shovel?"

Tyler avoided looking at Max's quizzical expression and instead cast his gaze out at the water's surface, wishing his mind felt as serene as the placid surface, the water barely bristling in the breeze dancing across it.

"You keep talking about money," Max said. "How much?"

Quinn faced his sister and looked her dead in the eye.

"One million dollars."

# NINE

Hatch sat motionless in the SUV. The rain had faded during her drive back to Portland, far from the tsunami-threatened coast, and gave way to a brilliant sunset that etched the clouds in pinks and purples, appearing more like cotton candy than the precursor to a potential disaster.

Not that she looked in her rearview mirror to see it.

The engine's hum disintegrated into nothingness after she cut the ignition. Staring out the windshield, she marveled at the mess she had left in her wake. Her clothes had yet to dry despite being out of the rain for over an hour, not that it mattered to her. She'd experienced far more uncomfortable conditions in the field, none of which had interfered with her ability to do her job.

Exiting the vehicle, she moved around to the passenger side and grabbed the clothes Jordan Tracy had given her earlier, then headed toward the lavish front entrance to the hotel. Entering through the revolving door, the giant lobby spread out before her. The twenty-foot ceiling was etched with swirls as a large chandelier twinkled from its center.

She made a mental note of the two entrances in the front, two at the sides, and one in the back hall, behind the concierge counter. There were no elevators in the immediate lobby, but she spotted three in the back hall. To her right, a dimly lit bar and restaurant was filled with well-dressed dinner guests and traveling business people unwinding with a drink after a day of meetings.

End tables, lounge chairs, and giant pots of foliage lined either side of the marble walkway to the concierge desk, all of which would become obstacles if something went wrong. Fire extinguishers were mounted on either wall. If there were emergency sprinklers on the ceiling, she couldn't spot them.

Hatch checked in at the desk and headed up to her room. Pressing the keycard to the magnetic lock, she heard a clicking sound as a small green light flashed.

Entering, she first grabbed a metal hanger before sweeping the closet, bathroom, and underside of the bed. She didn't have a gun on her, so the hanger was the closest weapon of choice. The hook could be used to penetrate or bruise when used creatively. Better safe than sorry.

Unloading her new wardrobe onto the closet rod, she found a small duffel bag with toiletries and another covered hanger with a note attached to the outside. It was from Cruise.

"Hatch. Meet me at the bar whenever you're ready. - C"

Unzipping the cover, she revealed a silk fire-engine-red evening gown, with one strap and a silhouette sure to hug her athletic curves. She found herself both admiring it and feeling appalled at the sight of it.

When was the last time she had worn something like this?

Had she *ever* worn something like this?

Hatch had never been the type to attend formal events. She'd attended award banquets, change of command ceremonies, and dining-ins to name a few of the military functions requiring her to wear her dress blues. But military formal wear and this dress weren't in the same league.

The dress would have to wait. Hatch was in need of a shower. A folded-up drying rack rested against the closet wall. Retrieving it, she stripped off the soggy clothes that had soaked her body to a prune, and laid them flat on the rack to dry. After starting the shower and letting it heat up, she stepped inside and let the water run across her skin. The day melted away along with the dirt and grime.

Intrusive thoughts about her encounter with Shyla broke the tranquility. Not to mention the ever-present turmoil regarding her past with Savage and her future with Cruise. Why was she so at odds? She'd learned on the battlefield that hesitation was weakness. A weakness that cost lives. Hatch had trained herself to make all decisions in a split second.

On the battlefield, she was most comfortable in her own skin, and outside of her mind. But when it came to communicating with those who deserved her attention, she was at a loss. The battlefield of emotion was one she'd yet to master, as if she'd ever given herself the chance.

Steam from the shower humidified the bathroom. She stepped into the makeshift-sauna which relaxed her muscles and softened her skin. After drying off with a soft white towel, she proceeded to her simplified beauty routine. Just as she'd never been one to wear evening gowns, she'd also never developed an affinity for makeup or hairstyles that took more than twenty seconds.

At the very least, she could work a blow-dryer on her long hair, and pinch her cheeks for a rosy undertone.

Returning to the closet, she slipped the evening gown over her slender frame and slid on the pumps Cruise had left underneath. A perfect fit, if not foreign wear to her. How Cruise had been able to eye the right clothing for her better than she could for herself, Hatch would never figure out.

Deciding her new attire looked as decent as it ever could, she grabbed her small wallet and room key and headed for the bar.

Cruise rose off his barstool when he spotted Hatch in the doorway. A smile crept over his face. His expression flashed desire as he took in her appearance. The scar tracing up her arm tingled as she was now overly conscious of it and its permanent meaning to her life. Even the battlefield never left her feeling this exposed.

"You clean up nice," Cruise said.

"Thank you, sir. Turns out you have better taste than I do." She offered a mock curtsey and smiled.

He leaned in for a kiss only for Hatch to turn her head, forcing his lips to land on her cheek. She kept her head turned as he held the small of her back and guided her to the spot he'd been saving. The liquor bottles on the wall twinkled, reflecting the lights above the smooth glass countertop.

Two bartenders stood behind the bar. One wiped down glasses and hung them in a hanging rack over the counter while the other waited on two customers seated to the right. Other patrons in business and eveningwear filled the wooden stools, leaving two empty ones for Hatch and Cruise at the end of the bar, facing the front entrance as well as a mirror reflecting the back of the restaurant.

He had already ordered drinks for them. The ice in her whiskey glass was formed in perfect cubes. He couldn't have ordered more than two minutes ago.

Cruise smelled of the ocean as she sat next to him, causing her mind to settle and then reel. She could let her guard down with him, but there was so much she hadn't said. That much he knew, too.

Cruise lifted his glass from the counter and motioned for Hatch to follow. "To us."

She clinked her glass against his without saying a word. They each took a sip.

She bit down as the burn slid down her throat. "How many drinks have you had so far?"

"Just one. Maybe two," Cruise said. "I got here an hour or so before you."

Nodding, she lifted her glass.

"How'd it go earlier?" he asked.

She exhaled a puff of whiskey-tinged air. "I ran."

"What do you mean?"

Feeling even more vulnerable now, at least she was telling some semblance of the truth. "I mean, Shyla reluctantly invited me in, and I told her I was the reason her husband was dead. Then tsunami sirens blared across the town, and I ran." She took another gulp of her drink and looked down at its contents as she swirled it against the bar.

"'I'm the reason your husband is dead' might not have been a great start," Cruise said, attempting to lighten the mood.

"It just wasn't the right time." Her shoulders slumped in defeat. "Seems like it never is. But I *am* the reason her husband is dead, and that is what needed to be said. I wish I could have explained what I meant. She deserves that much."

"Hatch." Cruise looked at her with an intensity that burned through her core. He laid his rough hand on top of hers. "Graham knew what he was getting into in that op. Like us, he knew what the cost was." He paused a beat. "He was a great husband and father, and one of my best friends. But you're the best operator I've ever seen, and your decision-making under fire is next to none. If *you* hesitated, anyone else would have, too."

His words sunk in. Hatch was unsure how she felt about Cruise trying to help her feel better when she was keeping so much more from him.

"Thanks." She moved her hand out from under his and placed it in her lap. Her gaze followed.

Cruise folded his arms on the glass counter. He looked back at her, presumably hoping she'd look at him too. That she'd really see him. Finally he mustered the courage to say what she'd been both dreading and expecting to hear for months. "Things have been off between us, Hatch. And maybe they've never really been…on. I don't know why. Maybe the reason doesn't matter."

Looking at Cruise while tracing her scar with her free hand, her heart thumped against her chest as she worried if he'd ask the question she'd not yet figured out the answer to.

Cruise continued. "You know that I love you. You can tell me anything. And you're not obligated to share your thoughts with me, but, you know, we're not on the field of battle. We can be real people when we're together. That's easier than being in the middle of combat, isn't it?"

He had no idea how much she wanted to agree.

"I love you too," she said at last. The words came with too much hesitation and Hatch could see Cruise registered the pause.

"I've been thinking a lot lately and I have something to propose to you."

She cringed inside at the word propose.

Cruise turned his whole body toward hers, and took her hands in his. She sat still, unable to focus on anything else as his warm palms surrounded hers. What was about to happen here? Her breathing quickened. Adrenaline shot through her. Whatever he was about to say to her, she wasn't ready for it. She'd prefer being in the middle of combat over this conversation any day.

"I don't think this is my calling anymore," Cruise said. "I'm ready to retire from the killing game."

Hatch exhaled, relieved that perhaps this didn't involve her. Maybe he'd say next that he wanted to retreat to a life of his own. Maybe she could let him decide her fate by going along for the ride with him.

"What brought this on?"

"I just think it's time to move on to the next phase." Smiling, he glanced down at the bar. His voice softened. "Hatch, I want to open a diner. And I want you to come with me. I don't want to hunt people down anymore. I want to be with you. I want us to start a real life. Be together forever."

*Forever.* That was a long time.

Processing his words, she stared into his breathtaking eyes. The world around her faded to black. The waves in her mind rose and began crashing over each other as though picking up the tide in a heavy storm. What if this was still her own calling?

Cruise let out a chuckle, an involuntary sort of sound that spoke to how relieved he was to have spoken his thoughts out loud to her.

"Come on, Rach. Let's open a diner together, *you and me.*" Cruise hummed a few bars of the Dave Matthews song with the same title as she recalled the two of them dancing in the dark to it on repeat. "We can live a normal life and have a normal relationship."

*Can I ever be normal? What the hell is normal, anyway?*

"Maybe we could retire to the California coast. Buy a property overlooking the Pacific. Serve coffee, beer, sandwiches, breakfast all day. Let's spend the rest of our lives together, living simply and happily."

*The rest of our lives.*

"What do you think?"

Hatch's throat caught. She couldn't think anything. The waves were getting bigger–as tall as a ten-story building–and they were filled with answers she couldn't bear to tell him. She couldn't stand thinking of how he'd react. Slowing her breathing, she brought the glass to her face. Oak and honey burned her nose. Another swig tried to calm her nerves.

She didn't want to pull away again, but she couldn't think about the rest of their lives. Not after Savage had said he'd wait for her forever if he had to. And damn him, too. How could she think about the rest of her life with Savage?

Unable to give Cruise the answer he wanted, and too terrified to offer the answer swimming in her gut, Hatch settled for her regular tactic as of late. Avoidance.

"We have to get through the next few days. Let's focus on that right now, okay?"

Defeated, Cruise let go of Hatch's hands and faced the bar once more. Hatch's heart wrenched as she watched his entire being fill with disappointment, gazing at the twinkling bottles of liquor behind the bar.

He turned just his head to face her one last time. "Just think about it. Please?"

"All right," she replied. "I'll think about it."

Cruise's phone vibrated at the same time that Hatch felt the alert notification on hers. Grabbing it off the bar top, he read the incoming message. It was from Tracy. The meeting was pushed to the morning. Suzuki has decided to spend the evening with his daughter. Cruise set the phone down. Flagging the bartender, with a wave of his fingers he ordered another round. "Looks like we've been given the night off. Might as well enjoy it."

Banyan bellied up to the bar beside Cruise. He had a big grin on his face as he slapped his former swim buddy on the back. "Hope I'm not interrupting."

Hatch settled in, grateful for the interruption. She met Cruise's smile with one of her own, and hoped it was enough to tide him over until she came to a decision.

# TEN

After an early breakfast, the team met Theo Clay in the hotel conference room as instructed. The room was large enough to accommodate a gathering of twenty people. The wooden oval-shaped table in the middle was surrounded by tan leather chairs. A large window encased the wall across from the door, allowing a perfect view of the city of Portland. The room had a door that separated them from the rest of the lounge, situated just across from the bar where Hatch and Cruise had met the night before.

After Cruise had told her he wanted to spend the rest of his life with her, and Hatch had avoided any commitment, they'd engaged in light small talk while they finished their drinks. Then Banyan joined them as they moved to a table and ordered dinner. They'd headed up to their rooms after eating and didn't speak for the rest of the night.

Hatch had stayed awake, letting the waves in her mind crash upon each other, eventually fizzling out to a calm lull. Not because she had come to a decision, but because sleep proved a more important venture.

Breakfast with the rest of the group had gone fine. Hatch had remained quiet and sipped her coffee, chiming in where she could, but let the men poke fun at each other with their usual banter before the business ensued.

Despite Cruise's initiative to be open and honest with Hatch, none of the tension from the prior months had dissipated. Hatch attributed this to her own indecision, and what she had put Cruise through. Luckily, the other men didn't seem to notice.

"I'm Jordan Tracy. This is my team, Alden Cruise, Ed Banyan, and Rachel Hatch. We're with Talon Executive Services." Tracy extended his hand towards Theo Clay, who shook it as though Tracy's larger hand were a grenade and applying any pressure to it would set it off.

"Pleased to meet you all." Clay's slicked-back, dark gray hair perfectly matched the smooth heather of his quality suit. His eyes glanced back and forth between the team behind thick-framed square eyeglasses.

Another well-dressed man entered the room. His dark hair was speckled with silver and groomed into a short quiff on his head. He walked with a cane and leaned some of his weight on it as he stopped to greet the group.

"Meet my boss, and the future of clean energy, Yohei Suzuki." Clay reached an arm out to pat Suzuki on his shoulder. "I have known this man for what feels like eons. We've worked together on a multitude of projects and business deals. So, keep him safe!" Clay laughed to suggest he was making a joke, although his eyes didn't follow.

Next, he gestured to a man who'd been standing to the side of the room since the team had entered. The team wouldn't have noticed him, had they not been well trained to notice their surroundings. "And this is my personal security, Parker Chase. You'll report to him for the duration of your time serving Mr. Suzuki."

Chase stepped forward and removed the shades which had hidden his eyes. He extended a much firmer hand to Tracy and the rest of the team. Even without the sunglasses, Hatch couldn't read his expression. He'd been trained to remain elusive and objective.

She wasn't bothered at the mention of being second in command to Chase. Tracy had let them know they'd be serving as backup, seeing as there were now two principals and a very large attendance expected for the speech.

Cutting any formalities and pleasantries, Chase began issuing orders. "The plan's a simple one. Experience has taught me the best ones always are." The comment earned a nod of agreement from the other operatives present. "We're going to roll out in a three-vehicle convoy. Tracy, take the lead SUV. Banyan, you'll bring up the rear in the other. Hatch and Cruise, you'll be with me in the limo, escorting Mr. Suzuki, Mr. Clay, and Mr. Suzuki's daughter, Akira." There were no objections from the group of seasoned veterans. Chase turned to Cruise, "I remember you helped Mr. Suzuki before?"

"That's right," Cruise replied.

"Very good. You know the drill then." Chase then addressed the team. "We'll be moving out in five minutes. The route takes us through Fairhaven, and then it's a straight shot to the decommissioned Trojan Nuclear site. Once we've arrived, you and Banyan will break off and park the SUVs in the volunteer lot and keep the engines running in the event we need an extraction."

"What's the distance from the volunteer lot to the venue platform?" Banyan asked.

"Approximately two hundred yards." Chase answered Banyan and then continued his instructions to the group. "We're going to bring the limousine to the side of the stage where the speeches will be made. Hatch, Cruise, and I will conduct close-in protection for our principals. I'll be with Mr. Clay. Cruise, Hatch, you'll cover the area in and around the stage. It's critical that a low profile is maintained at all times. Mr. Suzuki is very particular about this, so make sure you each blend in with the crowd.

"I'd also like to inform you we're looking at a crowd of approximately a hundred fifty attendees. And those not admitted will likely stand outside the gates and protest for the duration. The protestor numbers could reach in the hundreds as well. Local law enforcement has been assigned to maintain order and keep protestors far enough away. Keep your eyes peeled for any suspicious behavior. There are about a dozen or so activist groups who'll be doing their best to stir the pot."

"Great job, Chase," Clay said, forcing the other man to finish his directions. Clay's face contorted to something resembling sorrow, the sadness not quite reaching his eyes. "I'd like you all to know one more thing. Mr. Suzuki will give the speech in the place of another colleague, Frank

Dibner. You've been briefed on the situation with him, yes? He arrived at Fairhaven earlier than he was supposed to, and then dropped off the face of the earth."

The team nodded in response, exchanging glances at his blunt remark.

"Great." Clay nodded his head and clasped his hands in satisfaction, his sorrow vanishing. "Shall we be on our way?"

Chase led the group as Clay stepped in behind him and Suzuki followed, a little slower due to his injury. Hatch and Cruise took their places behind Suzuki on either side of him, in case he needed their stability.

As the team and their multi-millionaire cohorts moved through the lobby, a young girl bobbed up from a seat on the other side of the walkway and bound towards the group, her black hair shimmering side to side as she ran. She hurdled into Suzuki, nearly knocking him off balance. Hatch hurried to steady the man, releasing as quick as she'd held on as Suzuki welcomed the young girl with a one-armed embrace.

A split-second twitch of distaste landed on Clay's face. He'd recovered fast enough for no one to notice. No one except Hatch. "Ah yes, and this is Akira Suzuki, Mr. Suzuki's daughter."

Akira eyed the group, uncertain how to greet them. Hatch knelt to one knee, softened her eyes, and opened a palm for the girl to shake. "Hi, I'm Hatch," she said. "Your name's Akira?"

The girl nodded.

"That's really pretty," Hatch said.

Akira smiled as her cheeks turned pink, and she stood behind her father once again.

The group continued to move through the lobby's revolving doors and out to the awaiting SUVs and limousine, brought over by the parking valets a few minutes prior.

Chase turned to Tracy and Banyan. "You guys know where we're headed?"

"Yes sir, I've set up the address," Tracy said.

"Great. Let me give you all some earpieces so we can communicate." Chase reached inside the pocket of his coat and removed four small earpieces for each Talon team member. "They should be small enough for no one to notice. Remember, you'll want to blend in as much as possible. I'll make sure the parking attendants at the venue know you're security personnel."

The team nodded as they each took their earpieces and stuck them snugly in their ears.

Tracy and Banyan stepped into the driver's seat of their respective vehicles as Chase led Clay, Suzuki, Akira, Hatch, and Cruise to the limousine. He opened the door for the four and moved to enter the driver's seat.

Clay moved furthest in to a seat on the far side facing the doors, close to the front of the vehicle. Suzuki sat comfortably in the middle, avoiding getting too close to Clay's body, with Akira on his right. Hatch and Cruise took the back, facing the front as Cruise pulled the back door shut. The vehicle began to move. They could see Banyan following from the back window as Tracy took the lead in front.

Hatch and Cruise were sitting side-by-side, their legs and hips touching, and she could inhale his scent again. It almost took her from the moment, but Akira scooted a little closer to Hatch's left and began speaking.

"Ms. Hatch? Do you know how to do karate?" The young girl asked in her sweet, squeaky voice.

"Yes, I do." Hatch smiled and asked, "Do you?"

"No, my dad won't let me. It's how he hurt his knee." She eyed her father out of the corner of her eye. Hatch glanced in his direction. He turned his gaze away from the pair and looked out the window ahead of him instead. The highway was shrouded with trees, the occasional mountain popping up in the distance. Droplets of rain streamed down the windows, leaving trails in their wake.

"He won't tell me how it happened," Akira said.

Hatch turned her attention back to the young girl. "Maybe it's better that way. Sometimes we hold back so we don't hurt the ones we love most."

"I guess so." Akira sank in her seat, then popped back up again in a matter of seconds. "Do you have a gun?"

Hatch nodded.

"Can I see it?"

Suzuki and Clay's eyes widened at the request, both catching their breath and trying to fathom the words. Hatch spoke before either man got the chance.

"I don't think that's a good idea." At Akira's disappointment, she added, "I only take it out when absolutely necessary, and I only use it if someone puts someone else's life in danger."

Akira looked doe-eyed at the older woman, as if pleading with her for more explanation.

"Usually things don't get to that point. It's always better when situations don't end in violence."

# ELEVEN

"It is my great honor to introduce my colleague and friend, Yohei Suzuki."

Theo Clay stepped back from the microphone to exit the stage, stopping to shake Suzuki's free hand on his way to the podium.

The stage was situated on the coast of Fairhaven, lined by giant bristling trees and a waterline in the distance. A nuclear reactor could be spotted miles off the coast. The old Trojan Nuclear site. The ceremony was held outside in a gated venue. The rain had let up just in time for the event, although storm clouds still threatened the sky. White chairs were set up in front of the stage, filled by well-off congressmen and investors.

Protestors and newscasters clamored outside the gates, hoping to catch the attention of some attendee or another. At least, no one stood outside the gates wearing t-shirts or carrying a big neon sign that would indicate a threat beyond the obvious.

Hatch sat on the edge of the second row to the right of the middle aisle. Her teammates had spread out in the crowd in random seats after dropping off Clay and the Suzuki's behind the stage. Parker Chase stayed with Akira backstage.

Hatch surveyed the crowd in her peripheral vision, keeping a steady eye on the older Japanese man onstage. He looked so thin and frail, leaning against his cane for support, as though he could tumble at any moment. Hatch stayed at the edge of her seat in case she needed to bolt, though not so obvious that any seat neighbors noticed how she was—literally—on edge.

"Thank you," Suzuki started, allowing the applause to settle. "First and foremost, I'd like to acknowledge that I was not supposed to make this speech today. My partner in leading the change from oil to nuclear, Frank Dibner, was supposed to speak. Sadly, he could not be here today. I wish him the best, and I know his absence here is felt." He paused to ponder the crowd in front of him. "But you have me, and I am truly grateful to speak of the success and future of Aurora Nuclear." The crowd applauded again.

"As many of you know, we are standing on the site of a decommissioned nuclear facility. The iconic towers demolished in 2006 brought what appeared to be an end to Oregon's nuclear option. But I have a renewed vision for bringing back nuclear energy as a clean, cost-effective, and sustainable alternative. Using the newest technology, we're building an offshore transfer station that will receive its nuclear energy from a mobile flotilla, much like the Rosatom Project being used in Russia. We're already in the process of building our first vessel in Japan with plans of having it operational within a year. And if all things go according to plan, Aurora Nuclear will change the face of energy here in Oregon soon after." He looked over at his daughter. "My late wife told me that the future is in our hands. Let's not waste it."

A round of applause followed. Suzuki waited, soaking in the support that momentarily drowned out the protestors' jeers. He sipped from a glass of water and cleared his throat. "Nuclear energy has been villainized through its weaponization. But fear is usually the result of misinformation." Suzuki cast his gaze to the crowd gathered beyond the police barricade. "The energy harnessed from nuclear fusion is clean, and although not completely sustainable, it will be a bridge until other forms of alternative energy, like wind and solar, reach a point where they can match its output."

From somewhere in the crowd a protestor hurtled a bottle which landed in an aisle of the chairs, shattering on the concrete. Several attendees closest to the breaking glass gasped. The instigator was immediately snatched from the crowd by a group of law enforcement officers in riot gear. A small scuffle between several of the protestors trying to thwart the police extraction was quickly subdued. Hatch watched as four agitators were hauled away in flex cuffs. The crowd was building into a frenzy, but the cops held their ground.

Suzuki maintained his composure. "Fear contributes to ignorance. There have been many setbacks over the years. One in particular hit home for me. In 2011, the Fukushima Nuclear Power Plant in my homeland was devasted by an earthquake which sent fourteen-meter tsunami waves crashing down on the facility. Not since Chernobyl had there been such a disaster. It was from that incident that my idea of creating a safe alternative to the traditional model was born." Suzuki looked at his daughter. She smiled back. "By keeping the reactor on a mobile flotilla we'll be able to provide a level of safety unlike before. Our transfer station outside of Fairhaven will revolutionize our ability to deliver clean energy while maintaining a safe distance from population dense areas. Oregon will be the first to receive this service. In the coming years, Aurora Nuclear will be able to replicate its design, powering shoreline communities across the United States and the world. The future of clean energy is now."

Hatch listened to Suzuki's delivery while keeping a constant vigil on the faces and hands of those closest to the stage. She detected no threat. The supporters gave a standing ovation. The cheers were in stark contrast to those beyond the barriers.

When the gates opened to allow the newscasters in for a press conference, Suzuki gave them vague and general answers. Not wanting to give everything away while also not wanting to leave them without a story.

He disappeared through the back curtain to exit the stage. The crowd applauded and stood from their seats. They all made their way to the exit to the ceremonial grounds through the front gates, pushing against the unruly crowd. They were all headed to the boats that would take them to the reactor site where the ribbon-cutting ceremony would be held. Suzuki and Clay had planned to fly there on a helicopter and settle in before the crowd arrived.

Hatch and the team let the audience pass by them so they could slip behind the stage unnoticed.

"He's on the move." Parker Chase's voice cut into Hatch's ear. "Principal is on the move. Bring close-in support."

Hatch and Cruise met in the center aisle and made their way backstage to find the Suzuki's, Clay, and Chase. Chase had directed Banyan and Tracy to grab the SUVs and hurry back. The limo waited for its original five passengers next to the back exit. How they hadn't expected protestors and news teams to wait for Suzuki and Clay outside the back gate, Hatch didn't understand. Clay and the Suzuki's followed behind Chase as he led them to the limo. Hatch and Cruise fell in behind.

Chase opened the limousine door for everyone to step inside. Clay did so as Suzuki stopped to answer a question from a reporter on the sidelines. Protesters shouted all around them. Hatch could barely make out a word Suzuki said. Newscasters crammed their microphones and video cameras into Suzuki's face. Cameras clicked and bulbs flashed all around them. Clay tried to hurry the other man along, but Suzuki couldn't hear him.

Gasps and screams sounded from the back of the crowd. Chase abandoned the Suzuki's and his station at the car's back door to rush to a woman who'd collapsed on the ground, clutching a hand to her chest. Hatch and Cruise were met by a blockade of panicked onlookers. With Chase occupied, Hatch and Cruise began pushing through the crowd trying to make up the gap between them and Suzuki.

A white panel van pulled up behind the limo, its tires squealing as the driver slammed the brakes to a grinding halt. A male and female in caterer sweaters launched themselves out of the back side door. They were both hooded, so their faces were not easy for Hatch to make out. The female attacker swiftly snatched Akira from her father and threw the girl into the van.

Hatch knocked down one of the attendees as she barreled forward. She stumbled and caught herself, drawing the subcompact pistol from the small of her back. She didn't have a clear shot and kept the weapon low alongside her hipline as she bolted for the van.

The male, a little older than his female counterpart, was almost as tall as Hatch, though stockier. There was a grim look of determination and aggression on his face as he shot toward Suzuki, grabbed him by the waist and yanked him through the open van door.

Hatch had missed her window to save the Suzuki's from being abducted. In a last-ditch effort, she ran to the front of the panel van, placing herself between the kidnappers and their avenue of escape. She brought the Glock up, raising it to her target, taking aim at the driver. Pointed at the center of his skull, right between the eyebrows, she placed her finger on the trigger. Time moved slower, or at least the perception of it did, as the front sight oscillated in sync with her breath. She pulled the slack from the trigger, feeling the breakpoint.

In that moment, she looked into the driver's sunken eyes. Fear etched across his face as he prepared for her to shoot. His knuckles turned white as he gripped the steering wheel. He was as frozen as a deer in headlights. His eyes locked on Hatch and the weapon in her hand.

Upon recognizing him, Hatch lowered her gun.

She heard the van door shut. The driver seemed to wake up from a trance as he shook his head and his eyebrows knit together. He punched the gas pedal and maneuvered the large van around her. She'd spared his life, so it was only fair he spared hers, too.

She stepped to the side as the van whizzed by. The conflict of her decision punched her in the gut.

Tracy and Banyan followed the van down the road in the SUVs. Tracy lined the right side of the van as Banyan took the rear. They each fired multiple rounds at the windows, hitting the side panels instead. They missed their targets, the abductors.

They missed their opening, too.

The van's back door burst open. Another male caterer stood to the side of the opening, directing his gun at Banyan's SUV, then at Tracy's. More shots fired from both SUVs but missed as both men had to focus on driving and shooting at the same time. Just before disappearing around a corner, the predator got off two shots. One in Tracy's front tire. The other in Banyan's.

The SUVs both came to a crumbling halt, Banyan's nearly crashing into the back of Tracy's.

A large crackle came from the side of the stage. Everyone's attention shifted to the sound. Fire spread through the field as the whole stage went up in flames, the noise of the crowd drowned out by the distinct roar.

Hatch watched as the van escaped.

# TWELVE

THE CROWD HAD DISSIPATED AFTER THE FIRE HAD ENGULFED THE STAGE AND gunshots had flown back and forth down the road. They'd all escaped to the safety of their vehicles and presumably to their homes or hotels. The ribbon-cutting ceremony was effectively canceled.

"Hatch!" Cruise yelled with a bewildered look in his eye, his body tense. Crossing the sidewalk between them, he gestured with his arms wildly. Shrugging his shoulders, he put his hands on top of his head, then slid them down his face. "Hatch, you fucking had them." He covered his face in his palms. His voice sounded muffled, but she could still hear his words. "You had your finger on the trigger."

Dark clouds loomed above the scene, melding with the black smoke rising from the stage just on the other side of the gate. The rain hadn't been enough to diminish the fire. Sirens blared around them as the team of firefighters hosed the fire down and delegated one another for different tasks. The burning smell wafted over to Hatch with the wind. This was no nostalgic scent of a campfire. Burning metal, plastic, other non-wooden material carried more of a chemical scent.

Hatch barely processed her partner's words as she staggered back onto the sidewalk. What had she done? The thought process had seemed simple, reasonable at the time. Then again, she hadn't really paid attention to her thought process in the moment.

"Why didn't you just shoot? Don't you realize they now have the people we were supposed to protect?"

What was the matter with her? She'd been ready. Had her shot lined up. She'd let her morality get the better of her. Another split-second hesitation before she'd fully recovered from the last. One thing and one thing only had stopped her.

She'd recognized the driver.

If she'd killed him, there'd have been dire consequences, even though not killing him seemed to carry bigger ones. She could have shot the tires like his cohorts did to the SUVs. Or she could have just shot the passenger side of the windshield to spook him. There'd been other avenues than killing him. But she'd just stood there, imagining the aftermath of taking his life.

Cruise folded his arms and looked away from her. She'd spared someone's life, but had let her team down.

Tracy and Banyan were still down the road with their SUVs, patching the tires that had been shot by the extremist environmentalist group.

Theo Clay exited the safety of his limousine, pointing a finger at Hatch. "You! You let them get away. My colleague and his daughter, you let them get kidnapped. Unbelievable."

Cruise dropped his disgust towards Hatch long enough to insert himself into the confrontation. "And where was Parker Chase?" He gestured to the one-man security team.

Chase stood by, not acknowledging the standoff in front of him. He stood still, calm. His hands were clasped in front of him and his sunglasses shrouded any expression as though he wasn't even listening. The woman he'd assisted earlier was now loaded onto a stretcher in a paramedic van, traveling to the nearest hospital. If she had faked that heart attack, she didn't let up the act in front of anybody.

"Don't you drag my security into this. I think from here on out, we can handle ourselves just fine on our own. Your services are no longer necessary." Clay tugged on the opening of his suit jacket, as if it had been wrinkled from all the commotion. "Chase, we're leaving."

Chase peeled away from the sidewalk and headed to the limo, opening the door for Clay. Sliding in behind the fuel tycoon, he shut the door without a word. Hatch could no longer see the men through the tinted glass. The limo drove off in haste, leaving Hatch and the Talon team in their dust. The limousine traversed the same path as the panel van had, gliding down the building-lined road and rounding the nearest corner at the tallest gray skyscraper.

Hatch blinked at the scene around her. The hosed-off stage was now a mountain of disintegrated material. Tracy and Banyan finished patching the tires. They ran to Hatch and Cruise after seeing the limousine blaze down the road.

"Hatch, what happened back there? Looked like you had those guys." Tracy looked at her with disbelief, although with more empathy than Cruise had shown.

Cruise had reverted back to a standoffish demeanor. He stepped a few feet away.

"I just couldn't shoot the driver." Hatch looked down at her feet, and then at her scarred arm. A reminder of her hesitation at its finest.

"What now?" Banyan asked. "We just let everyone get away? Leave the op right then and there? Clay clearly doesn't want us involved anymore."

"No," Tracy said. "We finish what we started, and we find the Suzuki's. I've never let a client get kidnapped before, and I'm not about to let them get away now."

"Jesus Christ, if you had just pulled the trigger, we wouldn't have to find them!" Cruise said, finally looking at Hatch again. "I can't believe you, if you had just—"

"The driver was Graham Benson's brother-in-law." Hatch didn't try to keep the anger and impatience out of her voice. Just the other night Cruise had told her what a great operator she'd been in the field, saying that letting Graham die was what she'd had to do. Now, he was chastising her for hesitating. She'd had her reasons, and she was finally in her body enough to explain them.

Cruise's expression softened. He, Tracy, and Banyan exchanged sympathetic glances, eventually landing back on Hatch.

She let her head hang. "I couldn't shoot him, because I'd already taken one person from Shyla Benson and her daughter." Pausing, she looked the rest of the group in the eye. "I just couldn't take another."

# THIRTEEN

After a half hour of driving in start-and-stop rain, Tyler pulled the panel van into a large vacant warehouse space. Inside was nothing other than a few pallets of boxes and an assortment of other vehicles, so he pulled the van in as far as it would go.

Tyler's mind hadn't yet caught up to the present reality. They had just kidnapped not only another millionaire, but also his young daughter.

Quinn and Max exited the vehicle. Tyler stayed put and stared out the windshield in front of him as he listened to their muffled argument.

Max reeled at her brother's decisions as though she had no part in them at all. "First guns, now we're kidnapping these guys and their *daughters*? What the hell's gotten into you?" She raised her hands above her head. Tyler couldn't see her face, but her voice was loud enough. "I never agreed to anything like this? This is a felony. We could go to prison if we're caught. Or worse."

"We won't go to prison," Quinn said, as he started walking away from her. "And we won't get caught."

"You say this is about changing the world. You say this is about saving mom. You say a lot of things, but I think the only thing you really care about is that money."

"That money?" Quinn's voice rumbled like distant thunder. "How much was mom's last medical bill? How much will her next one be, and the one after that? You don't want to help, fine, then don't bother showing up to her funeral because you'll be the one responsible for her death."

Max followed Quinn as he walked away from her. "I get wanting to take the CEO, but what about the little girl? I don't see why—"

Quinn came to a grinding halt behind a large pile of boxes. Max almost crashed into him. Tyler watched Quinn in his driver's side mirror. His face was stone. His voice lowered and Tyler could barely make out the next words out of Quinn's mouth. "The best way to end a king's reign is to remove him and any heirs to his throne. It's time to either put up or shut up."

Max remained still as she shut down, watching her brother in shock. Tyler could see the side of her face and read her expression from what felt like a mile away. Max and Tyler seemed to be in the same boat. Neither had agreed to this level of destruction and protest against oily conglomerates. But how could they get out of it now?

Quinn stepped to the side as his other cohorts removed Suzuki and Akira from the back of the van, supervising them to make sure they moved the father and daughter to the other van, the one under Max's name. The gang had tied Suzuki and Akira with rope at the wrists after initially abducting them.

Suzuki remained stoic and poised. Emotionless. Akira shook with violent sobs as rivers ran down both sides of her round cheeks.

Tyler breathed deeply before leaving his driver's seat, letting the door slam behind him.

Max approached him once her brother's back was turned. She held her elbows in her hands. Tyler could plainly see she didn't like where this venture was headed. "Did you know this was part of the plan?" Max asked, her eyes moist and pleading.

"No." Tyler shook his head slowly. "I guess you didn't either."

"No." She motioned to her van, which Quinn had designated as their getaway vehicle.

"What do we do now?" Tyler asked. "Quinn's gone off the rails, and if we try to talk some sense into him, he'll make sure it's the end of us." Tyler swore he saw tears develop in Max's eyes, but they iced over before having the chance to fall.

"I know my brother's not a saint," Max said. "But I never would have imagined him to do something like this. I also know he's got a record, but he's never spoken to me that way or threatened me at all."

They looked over at Quinn and his minions gagging their captives, binding their ankles with rope, and throwing burlap sacks over their heads. They'd have no idea where the group would take them, nor where they'd end up.

Max covered her mouth. "I guess I was waiting for Quinn to stop, to tell us that it had gone too far, that all this was a desperate mistake. But here we are. To say that this has gotten out of hand is an understatement."

"How do we make it right? What do we do now?" Tyler asked again.

Quinn stood by the back of the van where their captives were secured. He rubbed his hands together with a smirk of satisfaction, as if reveling in the fact that the next step in his plan had come to fruition.

Neither Tyler nor Max acknowledged him, avoiding eye contact altogether. Tyler let out an exasperated sigh and exchanged a side glance with Max. He could feel the tension rippling off her.

"Aw, lighten up. Nobody's hurt. When all this is over, we'll be swimming in money." The taillights cast Quinn's face in red. Dark shadows danced under his eyes. The intensity of which told them that this was not over yet.

Even if they got away with the abduction and ransom, Tyler knew this would never be over. They'd be hunted. Forced to look over their shoulders for the rest of their lives. And then there was the matter of Frank Dibner. Tyler had heard the tone in Quinn's not-so-veiled threat earlier. Dibner was Quinn's leverage. He knew by involving Tyler, he'd locked him in. His servitude was out of self-preservation.

Quinn peeked inside to look at his captives. Then, he turned to Max. "Get in."

"Where are we going now?" Max asked. The defiance she'd shown moments earlier had all but dissipated. She tossed one last look at Tyler before steeling herself and sliding into the back beside the captives.

"I'm driving this time. You get to sit in the back." Quinn smiled coolly at Tyler, lifting his chin arrogantly and folding his arms against his chest. Tyler hesitated. He balled his fists and readied himself to stand up to Quinn. But when he opened his mouth to speak, nothing came out. Tyler relented and took a seat on the other side of the captives.

Quinn laughed at the younger man, then spoke to his prey. "Hope you guys don't get motion sick. Because those bags aren't coming off."

The side door slid shut, and the van zoomed out of the warehouse.

## FOURTEEN

Hatch found herself back in Shyla Benson's driveway. The rain had let up and given way to an overcast glow across the sky. Cruise sat beside her in the driver's seat. He'd driven her here for moral support.

Cruise had let go of his resentment toward Hatch's mistakes earlier that day. His mind had reeled in the moment because the criminals had been right there, in front of her, and all she'd had to do was pull the trigger. But after her explanation, he seemed to calm down. They were both thinking more clearly now.

"Are you ready?" Cruise asked her.

"I have to be," Hatch replied.

Responding with a curt nod, he turned off the vehicle. Stepping out of the car without looking back, she headed toward the familiar porch and front door, feeling as though it had been years since she'd last been here.

But it had only been a day.

Knocking on the door, she stepped back a foot.

Shyla's mother opened it and faltered. The older woman's long gray hair framed her face as it draped over her shoulders. Her hazel eyes widened in shock at Hatch's presence. "Rachel, I wasn't expecting you back."

It always threw Hatch when people referred to her by her first name, but she didn't bother to correct the older woman. There were more pressing matters to attend to. "I'm sorry I didn't call first. I was wondering if Shyla was around? I need to ask her about something."

"No, she's working at the diner. And to be frank, I'm not sure she wants to see you again." The woman leveled Hatch with a steely gaze.

Hatch felt her skin warm, though she didn't allow the woman's stance to intimidate her into breaking eye contact. She could take responsibility for the havoc she'd caused. "I know. I'm sorry about that too. But something's come up, and it's important I ask her about it."

"Well, you can find her at the diner if you really need to."

"Thanks," Hatch said.

Shyla's mother nodded in acknowledgment, and slowly shut the door without another word.

Hatch couldn't blame the older woman's reserved demeanor. She'd really dropped a bomb yesterday and hadn't even attempted to clean up the mess. Hadn't stayed to make sure everyone was ok, and she hadn't called or sent a message.

But all that would have to wait.

Hatch paced back down the driveway and opened the passenger door. Taking her seat, she looked at Cruise. "Are you hungry?"

---

CRUISE PULLED the car into the small lot right outside the diner. The name above the door read Crackers. Hatch felt her heart sink. She knew the meaning behind it. Graham's nickname. It was something Shyla had called him when they first started dating and it stuck. Now the handcrafted sign swinging gently above the door served as a reminder of the husband and father, and the operator Hatch had called friend.

The exterior was simple—red brick and a black roof. It could have been a renovated home. Two large windows rested beside the front door, parallel to a small porch lined with steps. Hatch could see patrons sitting inside through either window, laughing, sipping their coffee, and munching on donuts and pancakes.

Hatch and Cruise headed for the front door.

The diner was filled with local residents and travelers passing through. Hatch could hear chatter meld together with the occasional clinking of silverware and coffee cups. Upon entering, they noticed a familiar face standing behind the front counter.

Shyla Benson charmed her customers as she poured them coffee and took their orders. Her eyes were still red and puffy but soft as she engaged in pleasant conversation with her patrons, the edges wrinkled from smiling. Hatch wondered if the woman's cheeks hurt. Maddie sat at the other side of the counter drawing a picture, oblivious to her mother's presence. Her feet dangled off the seat, and she ticked her head back and forth, as if listening to her favorite song in her mind.

Hatch took a deep breath, and she and Cruise headed for the two empty seats at the counter. He placed a hand on her back, between her shoulder blades. It comforted Hatch at the same time it confused her. Assuming he wanted to let her know he was there, if anything went wrong, but after the anger in his voice earlier, she couldn't help but feel it was an empty gesture.

Shyla's back was turned to them now as she refilled the coffee pot. Three others were mostly full, presumably to use when any of the others ran out. She took up one of the full pots and grabbed a handful of silverware, heading on a mission to service a table on the other side of the counter. Shyla stopped in her tracks when she turned around and spotted Hatch and Cruise. Her skin turned paler than it had been, and her eyes hardened.

"You're back," Shyla said matter-of-factly, her eyes drifting to Cruise. "And I see you've brought company?"

"I'm sorry for showing up like this. But I have something urgent to discuss with you."

"Urgent? I saw you yesterday, and you–" She glanced over at Cruise, not wanting to involve the man. "Well, you said something I still can't quite wrap my head around. And then you just left. Who does that? Who drops a bomb like that and walks out? No explanation. Nothing."

"I know." Hatch shook her head as though trying to shake the memory out of it. "And I'm really sorry for that, too. But this isn't about yesterday. I know I need to explain what I said, but it'll have to wait. I'm here about your brother."

"Tyler?" Shyla set down the pot of coffee and silverware. She approached Hatch and Cruise, placing her hands on the counter and allowing her shoulders to shrug up to her ears. "What's he gotten himself into?"

"You might want to sit down," Hatch said.

Shyla looked down and took a breath. "Alright," she relented, then took up the full coffee pot.

"Care for a cup?"

Hatch and Cruise nodded. Shyla proceeded to grab three mugs from a shelf behind her and fill each to the brim with piping hot coffee.

She took the seat that had been vacated beside Cruise with Hatch on the other side of him. He scooted back to allow the women to face him and each other.

"Now, what's going on?"

Hatch took a sip of her drink before beginning. "We were tasked with protecting some pretty important people, and–" she paused, realizing little Maddie was only a few seats down and could hear every word of their conversation. "Well, they're involved with Aurora Nuclear. And we saw Tyler, um, protesting. Not so peacefully. Would you happen to know anything about that?"

Shyla's eyes began to gloss over, forming tears. She looked away from Hatch, down at her untouched coffee mug. "I don't know anything about what he does, no. He works here part time, but lately he's been away more often. I haven't seen him much in the last couple of months."

"So, there's no chance you know where he is now?" Cruise asked.

"Probably with Max," Maddie's little voice chimed in. She continued to draw her picture with a tiny grin perched on her face, her legs still dangling beneath the counter, making her torso wiggle.

"Max?" Hatch asked. "How does Tyler know him?"

"Not a him, silly." Maddie giggled. "Max is a girl."

Shyla eyed her daughter in concern. "How do you know so much about Max, sweetie?"

"I found a lot of crumpled up papers around Tyler's floor, and I uncrumpled them and saw a bunch of letters he wrote to her." The girl's soft cheeks turned a bright shade of pink.

"Do you know anything else about Max?" Hatch asked.

Maddie looked up from her drawing and thought for a moment, putting a finger to her chin and raising her gaze to the ceiling. She looked back at them and nodded once when she had her answer. "I know that she has red, red hair."

"Well, that narrows it down," Cruise muttered. Hatch elbowed him in the rib, causing him to nearly fall off the stool. He glared at Hatch, who'd turned away from him to sip her coffee and take on an expression of false innocence.

Cruise cleared his throat. "What else do you know?"

"Like what?" The girl giggled again and continued to draw her picture.

"Maybe her full name?"

"Oh." She paused, scrunching her nose and lifting a colored pencil to her chin, thinking hard again. "I think it's Maxine Russell!"

# FIFTEEN

Yohei and Akira Suzuki sat together on a cold, hard bench in the cabin of a small motorboat. Very little light shone down in the compartment, as daytime gave way to dusk. Droplets of rain seeped in through the grate overhead, landing on the wooden floor of the small compartment. Suzuki and Akira had heard the constant dripping throughout their travel so far. Waves jostled the boat around, causing Akira and her father to crash into each other.

Their bags, the bindings, and the gags had all stayed in place during the transfer from the van to the boat. If Suzuki had to guess, he'd say the drive to the boat had taken about half an hour. He had no watch or light to reference the time of day, but they were captured late morning, and the drive to the warehouse had taken an hour or so, give or take. Not that any of this was going to give him any leverage in saving his daughter from these thugs.

Loading on to the boat didn't take long, but he hadn't been able to figure out what the crew above were doing after they moved him and his daughter down a short flight of stairs.

When the boat had finally moved, Suzuki had felt himself become nauseous. He'd begun to salivate and swallow involuntarily, his stomach lurching. He willed himself to keep any bile from rising, mainly because it would all land in the bag over his head. Although vomiting wouldn't have been the way Suzuki had wanted to spend his time, anyway.

Still with bags over their heads, neither could see the other. Suzuki longed to continue comforting his daughter. It hadn't taken him long to realize the gag in his mouth had been secured improperly. He expanded his jaw wide and forced his chin up, allowing the cloth to move down and around his neck, freeing him to finally speak.

Taking deep breaths, he'd verbally reassured Akira, as much as himself, that they were fine and everything would work out the way it was supposed to.

Of course, he wasn't sure how everything was supposed to work out.

"I'M RIGHT HERE, SWEETHEART." Akira sat against Suzuki, pressing the side of her body to his. He tried brushing his arm against hers as much as he could, moving it back and forth slightly as both their wrists were still bound by rope. "Everything will be okay."

Akira squirmed against him and let out soft groans. She was struggling. She moved away from him, and he could no longer feel her touch.

Suzuki had failed her, he thought. If he'd just stayed quiet about his money, his investments, they wouldn't be in this mess. He should have done a better job of keeping her safe. Maybe if he'd taught her karate like she'd always wanted, it'd be enough for her to defend herself. Maybe after this was all over, he'd finally make her wish come true. If something like this happened to her again—and as the heiress to a billion-dollar fortune, it very well might—he'd want her to be able to defend herself. Would she be able to, at her size and age? Perhaps not. But he wouldn't have to live with the guilt that he never let her learn. Never gave her a chance.

Lord knew he couldn't, as much as he wanted to. Having permanently damaged his knee years ago, in doing so, he'd permanently damaged his ability to fight ever again.

Feeling the weight of these thoughts, Suzuki let his head fall and his chin bounce against his chest, not realizing the burlap sack over his head would slide right off. *Amateurs.* He let it fall to the ground, and immediately tried to find his daughter, assuming she'd moved just out of reach.

But she was no longer sitting at all. Had the captors snuck down without him realizing it and taken her from him?

After a split-seconds panic, Suzuki realized his daughter now stood in front of him. The bag no longer covered her head. The gag had fallen all the way down her neck, and her binds were loose. Shock and relief flooded him.

"How did you—"

"It doesn't matter," she said. "Let me get the ropes off you." Akira slid her hands behind her father's back and began to work on his binds.

"We have to get out of here," Suzuki told his daughter. "There's only three of them. When I make my move, I want you to stay out of the way. I will only get one chance."

Suzuki was grateful his kidnappers hadn't tossed his cane during the abduction. His crutch would now become his saving grace. His weakness would become his weapon.

The boat came to a stop, and its motor cut off shortly after. All they could hear was the sound of waves crashing against the boat and the light pitter-patter of rain. Less seeped through the grate and landed on the floor now. It had slowed to a drizzle. They tried to stand still as the waves jostled them. Suzuki steadied himself with his cane. They heard a single set of footsteps above. Then, a voice.

Suzuki and Akira readied themselves to launch out through the grate, careful not to alert anyone to their presence under it.

"Excuse me, sir, would it be alright if we docked here?" the voice of one their captors asked. His voice carried over the waves slapping against the side of the boat. "The storm knocked out our comms and radar, so I couldn't find the way back to shore. Can you call a tugboat to pull us back in?"

Suzuki felt his daughter slide behind him, seeking his protection. Her small frame quaked with fear. Whether it was the fear in his daughter, or his own, Suzuki's confidence began to wane. He could feel his heart slamming inside his chest and fought to conceal his nerves from Akira.

Another voice sounded above. Older. Gruffer. "This is a restricted facility."

"We won't be any trouble, there's just three of us."

Silence ensued for a few more seconds.

"Alright," the older voice said. "You can tether up, but you'll have to remain down here at the dock. And I'll see what I can do about getting you a tow."

"Thanks."

Suzuki turned to Akira. "I want you to stay down. Don't come out unless you hear my voice." Seeing the fear in his daughter's eyes, he hoped the darkness veiled the fear in his own.

"I'm scared." Akira's body shook.

Suzuki gripped the cane. "I know. I am too." Bending over, he kissed his daughter on the head. He thought of his wife. He thought about what he was about to do now and worried he would leave his daughter alone in the world. The thought sickened him, and he fought back another urge to vomit.

Akira tucked herself into the farthest corner as Suzuki readied himself. It was only a few steps up. He'd have to move quickly and quietly. The element of surprise would be his best advantage. There'd been one who seemed to be in charge. Suzuki would target him, hoping to gain the advantage. Plus, he was no longer alone. The security guard helped to level the playing field.

Suzuki was crouched low and made his way to the bottom of the stairs leading to the upper deck. In the dark, he reached out for the railing just as a wave crashed into the side of the boat. The violent jerking sent Suzuki sideways. He lost his footing and fell against the hull. The cane slid out from under him and slammed against the wooden floor with a loud *thwack*.

"What was that?" the security officer asked.

"Shit," the leader said.

Suzuki was scrambling to his feet when a gunshot rang out.

## SIXTEEN

After finding out about Maxine Russell, Hatch and Cruise had contacted Jordan Tracy with the name. He'd used his resources to investigate her. He and Banyan had gotten to the diner about an hour after Hatch and Cruise had called. In the meantime, Hatch and Cruise had sipped their coffees and theorized about what was going on.

When Tracy and Banyan arrived, they had moved from the counter and taken up a booth to fit the four of them. Shyla came by every so often to refill their coffees. She'd been all too happy to finish the conversation about Max and Tyler and distract herself with her work.

As the four settled in, Shyla came by once more with her coffeepot. "Can I interest you all in a meal? I'm starting to think you'll need it."

"What do you suggest?" Hatch asked, not disagreeing.

"You should try out the snow crab platter. Comes with a side of clam chowder, garlic bread, melted butter, cocktail sauce, and steamed vegetables."

"That sounds great."

"Should I grab four?"

The rest nodded. Shyla glided back to the kitchen to put in their order.

Tracy sipped from his mug and set it back down.

"What'd you find?" Hatch asked.

"Maxine Russell is in her mid-twenties, dropped out of med school. She's involved in an environmentalist group called The Watch. They're a small group mostly involved in protest movements. No acts of violence. Vandalism is their main weapon. Until now." Tracy continued. "She was arrested about a year ago for graffitiing a bunch of gas stations, but served no time and only received community service."

"I wonder how Tyler got mixed up in this?" Cruise said. "Shyla said he was a good kid?"

"Maybe a crush," Hatch said. "People do a lot of stupid things for love." Thinking about her word choice, she regretted it the moment she met Cruise's eyes.

"I did a little more digging on The Watch. I think it'll connect some of the dots. The group is led by Quinn Russell."

"Her brother." Hatch's eyebrows furrowed.

"Right. He's thirty and has a hefty record on him. Petty theft, armed robbery, served about three years in prison before getting out last year." Tracy paused to sip his coffee again. "He got involved in the environmental battle after getting out."

"And now he's added kidnapping to his resume. Sounds like he's building on his violence resume," Hatch said. "My gut's telling me if he hasn't killed anybody yet, he's going to."

Tracy nodded and pulled out a tablet from his bag and began tapping on it. "Here's the footage of the abduction. I did my best to unblur the faces, but it's not perfect."

The footage of the man and woman abducting the Suzukis played through, just as Hatch remembered it in real life. They were both hooded. The girl's deep red hair slipped out of her hood and into the frame as she wrapped her arms around Akira and tugged her into the open van, a detail Hatch had overlooked in the moment. Her face was still blurred out. Her male counterpart was more visible. Hatch studied the still frames on the tablet. She stared at the one image. It had to have been Quinn. Though she couldn't make out the details of his face, she could see his eyes. In them, Hatch saw the eyes of a killer. Cold and calculating.

"We also ran the van plate to see if either Russell owned it. No luck, but we did find out they switched out their vehicles to cover their tracks. My sources saw some other guys drive that panel van back the way they came. Retracing their steps, we figured out where they took the new transport vehicle."

The discussion paused as Shyla came brought over four bowls of clam chowder. Steam rose from the bowls as they devoured the thick soup. As soon as empty spoons clanked against the porcelain, Shyla was back with their entrées. Setting the plates down in front of them, she hurried away after they all murmured their thanks. The snow crab platter sent plumes of salty clouds into the middle of the table. Their scent wafted around and made Hatch's mouth water. Hearing her stomach grumble softly, she decided to dig in while Tracy continued relaying his findings.

"The other vehicle is Maxine's," Tracy continued. "We were able to track it close to the docks. Police have swarmed it and are checking for DNA as we speak."

"If they're not at the car, where could they be?" Hatch asked.

"They must be out on the water," Cruise said. "There's nowhere else for them to go."

"There's a real threat of tsunamis out here," Hatch said. "The Suzukis could be in danger, not just from the extremists, but also from nature."

Tracy began shoveling food into his mouth as though this would be his last meal for a long time. "Maybe we can catch them before a tsunami does."

"Maybe we should call Theo Clay and present that to him. Let him know we still care about this mission," Hatch said.

"On it." Banyan pulled his cell phone out of his pocket and dialed Theo Clay's personal line. As it rang, he pressed the button to put the call on speaker.

The ringing stopped, and a voice answered. "Clay."

"Mr. Clay, this is Ed Banyan with Talon. First, I want to apologize for what happened earlier today. It was truly egregious on our part to have allowed such an oversight. But I wanted to run a plan by you. We have a location on the abductors, The Watch, and can find them not far offshore."

Clay chuckled with contempt on the other end. "Why thank you, but there's really no need for your involvement anymore. My security and I have things handled from here on out."

"We can still help you," Hatch said, inserting herself. "If you give us a chance, we can prove to still be of service."

"I assure you, Ms. Hatch, that is really not necessary." She cringed at being called Ms. No one ever put Ms. Before her last name. "I plan to meet with the abductors at the reactor site to retrieve the Suzukis and give them money in exchange." Clay's voice stayed calm, measured. "All will be well, and your services are not needed. Thank you, I must be going."

He hung up before giving the team another chance to speak.

Banyan repocketed his phone and began to shove food in his mouth. His look of irritation was quickly replaced by satisfaction.

"Maybe we should still go for the exchange. Just to make sure nothing shady happens," Cruise said.

Tracy paused to finish his last bite of food before speaking. "Well, it's kind of out of our hands. We'd never get a helicopter in time, and even if we could grab a boat, they'd see you coming a mile away."

"Not if we're underwater." Banyan looked up with a wide grin on his face.

The four exchanged knowing glances.

"There's only one Draeger, so you'll have to buddy breathe. I will remain on the boat. I'll maintain my distance and keep watch." Banyan looked at Hatch and Cruise as he continued his meal, his eyes wide like an excited child on Christmas Eve.

"I'm going to remain shoreside and try to talk some sense into Clay. Maybe I can get him to delay this deal long enough for you to bring this thing to resolution." Tracy drained the remnants of his mug.

After the four finished their platters and last rounds of coffee, they paid for their meal and left through the front of the diner, waving goodbye to Shyla and Maddie. Hatch looked back at the woman one last time. Shyla met her eyes and gave an almost imperceptible nod. But Hatch noticed it and could decipher what it meant. The two women were on amiable terms. Hatch still needed to undo the damage of the other night, but that would have to wait.

A second after exiting, the sky opened up, dumping precipitation all over the parking lot and off into the distance. The group was sheltered by the overhead covering outside the diner.

Cruise gave Hatch his patented cocky smile as the rain fell more steadily. "As we used to say in the teams, if you're going to be wet, you may as well be underwater."

# SEVENTEEN

Lights shone down from the nearest support beam while Tyler sat with the bleeding guard on the dock. The man was fading in and out of consciousness, going back and forth from writhing in pain to complete stillness.

Max had gone back to the boat to retrieve something to soak up all the blood. Quinn had shot the man in the upper left quadricep, avoiding any major arteries. But with the amount of blood loss, the man was at risk of infection, or worse. Tyler ripped the end of his shirt to soak the blood in the meantime, realizing the man's life was more important than keeping his torso covered. All he could hear was the sound of his heart beating, the guard panting for breath, and the water lapping around the nuclear transfer facility.

Tyler couldn't see where Max had gone. It was chilly, dark, and drizzling. The water seemed like a large empty void that would swallow you whole and never spit you out if you jumped in. A deep black pit. The overhead light helped a little, but only in his direct line of vision. He could barely make out the boat at the dock right in front of him, let alone the coast miles away.

Max rushed back to them from the boat's dark abyss, her deep red hair blowing wildly from the run and the wind. Unable to find any more material to soak up the blood, she took over Tyler's job, applying pressure to the man's injury with Tyler's already blood-soaked shirt.

"How are you doing that?" Tyler asked her.

"Just have to press down a little harder than you think," Max replied. "Just enough to slow the bleeding if not stop it completely. I learned about the proper technique in med school, but it's pretty basic."

Tyler nodded in understanding.

Once the bleeding slowed down, the pained look in the guard's face fell away replaced by a blankness. He untensed the rest of his muscles and relaxed into sleep. Max released the heavy pressure and slumped against the wooden post on the dock.

Quinn stalked over with another man, one hand gripped around the maintenance worker's forearm while his other held the guard's assault rifle. He'd taken the rifle after shooting the man. He'd left Max and Tyler to deal with the aftermath of his impulsive decision and gone to find more people to terrorize.

The maintenance worker wore a hardhat and was bound at the wrists with rope and gagged by a white cloth. He gripped a first aid kit in his hands.

"Attention, maggots!" Quinn raised the rifle, pointing it up in the air, as though claiming some twisted victory.

Tyler looked over to the men, and Max launched out of her seated position, snatching the kit from the maintenance worker.

"Aggressive tonight, are we?" Quinn quipped.

Max ignored her brother, rifling through the kit. Tyler noticed the look of determination mixed with fury on her face. It amazed him how cute she looked at that moment.

Finding gauze, she went to work applying it to the guard's leg, gently lifting his knee and wrapping the gauze around his thigh. She gestured for Tyler to help her hold the cloth in place.

Turning her face away from her brother's line of vision, she whispered low enough so as to not alert him while he supervised them. "This was never part of the plan," she told Tyler, as much as she was telling herself. "Kidnapping people. Shooting people. He never talked about any of this.

We just agreed this would be the way to get money for our mom's surgery."

"Why would this be the way?" Tyler asked. Opting for a more casual tone. "Haven't you guys thought about, you know, finding actual jobs maybe?"

Max scowled. "It's not that simple. Not with our records." She turned her gaze back toward the guard's leg. "How can you say that when you're right here with us?"

Tyler's heart skipped a beat. She was right. But the truth was, he was there only because Max was there. Max was worth all of this. She had to be. He thought back to his brother-in-law again. He never would've gotten himself involved in something like this. And if by chance he did, Graham never would've let it get this far. But with each step forward, Tyler realized he was less and less like him.

Before Tyler could mentally answer his own question or verbally respond to Max, Quinn stomped over to the pair and interrupted. "Jesus, Max, we have things to do. We don't have time to sit around and fix people." The maintenance worker stood where the dock met the support beam, looking confused and bewildered. He tried to talk with the gag still in his mouth, his words coming out muffled and more like groans from not being able to move his tongue.

Max rose from the guard again and looked her brother in the eye. Tyler took over wrapping gauze around the guard's wound, but paid close attention to Max's confrontation with her brother.

"Quinn, you just shot somebody. He could have bled out and died."

"And?"

"Are you serious? You just got out of prison, and you're turning to this life again?" Max didn't try to hide the disappointment and anger in her voice. "What sick satisfaction do you get out of all this? What is your goal here?"

Quinn shouldered the rifle and stepped closer to his sister, his face inches away from hers. "*Our* goal. We agreed this was how we'd get the money for Mom. You can stay here and care for this stupid guy all you want and leave everything behind. But at the end of the day, the money matters. You know why we're here. Now, are you coming with me?"

Max looked at her brother defiantly. Her fists were clenched tight, and her shoulders were shrugged to her ears. As much as her mouth moved to say something, no words came out. Her gaze drifted down, and she stumbled back, as though Quinn had punched her in the gut.

Quinn smirked down at his younger sister. "I thought so." He relaxed with the rifle. "Glad we're on the same page. Plus, we'll probably have enough extra cash to put towards environmental causes. That's why we're all here, right?" Quinn looked pointedly at Tyler, still seated on the ground.

Tyler nodded in agreement, only glancing in Quinn's direction for a moment.

Quinn took on a new air of pep and reshouldered the rifle. "Great. Now let's get a move on. We have a visitor coming."

As he stepped away from Max, he punched the maintenance man in the side of the head, rendering him unconscious and giving the group one less person to worry about. Then he leaned down and gripped the hardhat that had fallen from the worker's head, placing it on his own. Quinn dragged the man to lay by the support beam on the dock. If anyone else showed up, it would be too dark to notice him lying there. He looked back and smiled at Tyler and Max like some evil villain. "You guys care about that guard so much, you get to carry him up the stairs." Turning back around, he headed for the nearest staircase.

The wounded man's eyes flickered. He was slipping in and out of consciousness. Tyler swallowed hard. He'd buried one man for Quinn and wasn't about to leave this man to die.

# EIGHTEEN

POLICE SWARMED MAXINE RUSSELL'S CAR AT THE DOCKS, MUTTERING among themselves about DNA samples and her and her brother's past records. Dark clouds loomed overhead, and the rain hadn't let up since the team left Shyla's diner. They were all drenched from having to wade through the rain to get in and out of vehicles.

Tracy's contact had driven up in a truck. He hadn't gotten out to say so much as 'hello' before Tracy picked the inflatable boat out of the back and the driver drove off. Tracy hadn't told the group his contact's name or where they'd known each other. It wasn't important.

Tracy had also quickly located wetsuits and flippers for Hatch and Cruise to help them prepare for their underwater mission. He'd given them each a firearm and a waterproof bag to carry the weapons and other supplies. Cruise wore the Draeger rebreather on his back. He planned to share the mouthpiece as well as the Swim Buddy with Hatch.

Once everyone was in the appropriate attire and ready to go, Hatch, Cruise, and Banyan piled into the inflatable motorboat. Capable of carrying up to six people, though not comfortably, it would transport them to their final destination and keep them out of the water until then.

Tracy had delegated himself to stay behind at the docks and try to get some intel from the police about Maxine and Quinn Russell.

"You guys remember how to use the Swim Buddy?" Banyan asked as they pulled away from the docks and began their trek across the Pacific. The nuclear transfer facility was about five miles through the water, and they could just see it beyond the rain. "It'll probably work best if you lay on it side by side and each press on a paddle to propel forward. And you guys can figure out between yourselves how to share the Draeger."

"Got it," Hatch said. Her eyes fell over the vast water surrounding them. The little light left in the sky was enough for her to make out each surrounding wave, but it wasn't as clear as it would have been in the daytime. "These waves are big. I'm surprised they're not overturning us."

"These are nothing," Banyan replied. "These boats are able to withstand waves up to ten feet high." They hit wave upon wave as they traveled farther into the ocean, the salty water splashing their faces and bodies. Hatch licked her lips occasionally, forgetting about the fresh coating of salt. The wetsuits, still damp, were enough to keep them mostly warm. Banyan had put one on as well, just in case. "Cruise and I know a thing or two about big surf."

Cruise smiled. "Our BUD/s class faced some challenging conditions. We were an El Niño winter class, pounded by twenty-foot shore breakers."

Banyan spoke loudly over the motor. "You never told her about that day?"

Cruise shook his head. "You tell it better."

Banyan began as if telling a campfire story. "On a dark and stormy day, not unlike today, our class was sent out to the surf for our mandatory two-mile ocean swim. We were already down to seventy-seven from the original one-forty that we started with. And these are tough guys, all of them, some better swimmers than others. Cruise and I were partnered, not for our height. But for our speed in the water.

On this day, we were both tested. It was like swimming into thunder. The crashing waves were so loud. We tried to time it. Best way to take the big waves is to swim under them, never by going over. When we did, we made it about halfway out. To do the two-mile ocean swim, you've got to swim past the breakers to the calm water, and then you travel along the shore, pass the Hotel Del down to the far end of the beach and then a mile back. We swam out about halfway when a massive breaker hit us. It drove me down so deep I couldn't find which way was up.

I swear to God, I hit the bottom of the ocean at twenty feet deep. But worse is it kept me pressed down. And then came the churn. The waves that came behind it sucked me up and spun me around. I fought my way back to the surface, but there was at least a foot, maybe more, of churned white-water froth, so when I broke the surface and tried to breathe in, I inhaled nothing but salty foam, choking on it and blinded by the tumultuous water around me. Another massive wave knocked me back underwater before getting a full breath. At that point, in the dark water, I had vertigo, couldn't find up or down.

And to be honest, I gave up. Thought it was over. Couldn't figure my way out, and so I figured I would drift. I had the wind knocked out of me by the second wave, and I'd inhaled a ton of water. I was losing consciousness. And then, like Poseidon's hand, Cruise found me and he pulled me out. He dragged me to shore. When I finally got my senses back, coughing up the water and collecting myself, I heard the sirens from the shoreline. The SEAL instructors had followed us in, saying the water was too dangerous.

But for the moment, we thought we were going to get a break, and then one of the instructors smiled. I'll never forget the look on his face. Through my facemask, standing there in the cold with rain pelting down on us, he smiled at us and he said, 'The only easy day was yesterday. SEALs are born in adversity. The ocean's calling you. Will you answer it?'

At that, he sent the others back into the surf, back into the thunderous waves crashing down on the shore. Cruise looked at me, and though neither one of us spoke, he saw the tears in my eyes, inside my mask, and all he said was, 'I'm your swim buddy. I'll see you through to the other side.' Ten minutes of hard swimming, we were the only two to make it through the shore breakers that day.

Something happened that day in the water. Can't describe it, but it was a turning point for me. It was the moment I realized I'm only as good as the guy next to me. Or gal."

"We were the only two swim buddies assigned from day one to graduate together," Cruise chimed in.

Banyan held out his fist for Cruise to bump. He shut the motor off after passing the larger waves into the calmer section of water, and determining they were close enough to the transfer site for Hatch and Cruise to swim it. "Seems like we're about a mile out, so I think you'll be able to make it in fifteen minutes or less. I'll wait here for your signal. If for some reason, we can't establish comms, just fire a flare and I'll be there in two shakes of a lamb's tail."

Clay's helicopter blazed over the coast and approached their location, heading for the reactor's landing pad. No one in the helicopter would have been able to see Hatch and Cruise in the water below—it was too dark at this point in the day. The boat was painted dark enough to not give off any reflection, either. The helicopter passed over them, continuing its path to the transfer station.

It was time.

Cruise took one last look at Banyan. "Let's do it."

"Good luck guys. Remember, just fire a flare if you need me."

Hatch nodded in acknowledgement as she and Cruise readied themselves to launch into the ocean.

The pair backflipped off the side of the boat. They swam out a few feet and came back up for one last breath of air. The two faced each other as they bobbed up and down from treading their legs in the wavy sea. Hatch looked into Cruise's cobalt blue eyes, staring right back into hers, contrasting with the dark features of nature around them. Her heart beat faster, or was that just from the temperature of the water?

"You ready?" Cruise asked her.

Hatch thought back to Banyan's story. *Ten minutes of hard swimming, we were the only two to make it through the shore breakers that day.*

"I have to be, but this is pretty new territory for me. I wasn't trained in the water much."

*...all he said was, 'I'm your swim buddy. I'll see you through to the other side.'*

"That's why we have a swim buddy." Even though she couldn't see his face clearly in the dim light, she could tell he was smiling at her.

The helicopter's thumping was the last sound they heard before diving under the dark water, toward the operation that lay ahead.

The cold darkness swallowed them. Underwater, Hatch heard Cruise's words in her head as the Swim Buddy propelled them forward. *The ocean's calling you. Will you answer it?*

# NINETEEN

QUINN HAD DISAPPEARED INTO THE FACILITY FOR A FEW MINUTES, SAYING HE wanted to check out the place and make sure the coast was clear. When he came back down, he'd ordered Max and Tyler to bind and gag the unconscious guard, and shuffle him and the rest of their captives to an engineering room upstairs. After providing these instructions, Quinn left them to again clean up his mess. He'd said he was going to find the helipad where he anticipated meeting the millionaire.

Max and Tyler did as they were told, binding the guard's wrists with rope and tying a white cloth around his mouth and neck. They left the other man at the dock to grab their other captives from the bottom of the boat.

They found the father and daughter already unbound, ungagged, and with no bags over their heads. Yohei Suzuki sat on the ground trying to find his footing with his cane, while his daughter helped him to his feet. The two looked shocked to see Tyler and Max, as if they thought they'd be down in the bottom of the boat forever. Suzuki got to his feet and stood in front of Akira, probably ready to whack their abductors with his cane at any moment.

Of course, Tyler's instinct was to not harm the pair.

"Please," Suzuki said. "If you have to take anyone, take me. Let my daughter go. She's just a child, she deserves to live her life. I've already lived mine."

A faint gasp sounded from behind Suzuki as his daughter took in her father's words.

"I'm really sorry about this, man." Tyler shook his head and averted his eyes from Suzuki's. "None of this was part of the plan. At least, Quinn didn't tell us it was."

"Quinn?"

"My brother," Max said. "We didn't know it was going to be like this. I'm sorry."

"Sorry doesn't make it right. Whatever he's paying you, I can double it."

Max and Tyler both bowed their heads in shame.

"Look," Suzuki said. "I've seen men like Quinn before. He has you two doing all of his dirty work and taking the brunt of it." The man sighed and let his guard down, just a little more. His grip on the cane loosened, but not enough so he'd fall. "Once he has whatever it is he's looking for, what'll stop him from harming not just me and my daughter, but also the two of you?"

"He's just in it for the money," Max replied. "That's the main thing keeping me and Tyler on board. But like he said, we never agreed to a plan where we'd harm either of you."

"That may be," Suzuki said. "But the look in his eyes was all too telling. Murder was written all over them. And once he starts, he will never stop." Suzuki's eyes blazed into his younger kidnappers.

Max and Tyler stared at the other man, knowing he was right. Tyler looked over at Max. Her expression was hardened and cold. He wanted to be able to read her mind, know what she was thinking at that moment. What did she think about her brother being a cold-hearted killer? About the fact that he seemed to be losing more of his mind by the second?

Akira poked her face out from behind her father, capturing a glimpse of her young abductors.

"We have to take you guys up now," Max said, ignoring the conversation and steeling herself.

Suzuki stood defiantly in front of them, but before he could say anything, Max softened. "You guys can't go anywhere else. We might all make it out of this alive, but if you don't come with us, you won't have any chance."

Suzuki relented, and Akira stepped out from behind him.

Max gently took hold of Akira, and Tyler took Suzuki to head back up the stairs into the rainy night. The man wrapped an arm around Tyler's shoulders, and Tyler held onto Suzuki's cane as they moved up the steps.

Ordering the Suzukis to stand at the bottom of the steps to the facility and wait while they got the guard, the pair didn't argue. Max and Tyler were able to lift the guard, but his weight was too much for them to carry. The man's legs dragged behind him as they moved to the stairs. Akira and Suzuki began to climb as Tyler and Max slowly pulled the heavier man up.

Out of breath, they reached the inside of the facility. It was walled off from the outside. Following Quinn's directions, they moved straight from the stairwell, took a right, and then approached a door on the left. The only light in the hallway came from the low-energy floor lights illuminating their path as they moved.

The engineering room had multiple windows, including one in the door, so they could see inside from the hallway. Suzuki and Akira had stopped beside it to let Max and Tyler pass with the wounded man.

"In here," Max said, nodding at the Suzukis for one of them to open the door. It took all of her strength to keep the guard upright. She also held the med kit in her free hand.

There were enough chairs for the four to sit. Max and Tyler set the guard down against the wall next to the door. They didn't bother restraining the Suzukis again. There was nowhere for them to escape to, no one they could call to for help. But mostly, Max and Tyler had made a silent agreement to do what they could to protect these innocent people.

A few moments after settling in, Quinn stormed through the door. He held one hand behind his back and one was still carrying the guard's rifle clasped against the front of his chest and shoulder.

"Greetings!" Quinn threw his head back as though this were the best day of his life. How excited he was to have captured people for a chunk of money! "So lovely to see you all. Tyler, will you join me for our cohort's arrival? And Maxy, you stay here with these folks. Make sure they don't try to steal our boat." Quinn smirked as he turned back out the door.

Max winced at the nickname. Tyler had learned she hated when people used it. Only her mother was allowed to call her that.

Tyler followed in the corrupt environmentalist's wake. "Where were you?"

"Just taking care of a little insurance plan." He tapped the inside of his jacket pocket, his lips curling into a half smile.

"Insurance plan? What does that mean? Is our guy here?"

"No, not yet. All in due time."

"I'm involved in this more than I'd like to be. Tell me what the hell is going on."

Quinn reached his hand into his pocket and pulled out a small black box that looked like an old flip phone. He held it in the palm of his hand.

"What the hell is that thing?"

"Like I said. It's going to guarantee our way out of here. And trust me when I say this, you'll thank me later."

"You still didn't answer me."

"It's a remote detonator."

"For a bomb?" Tyler stumbled back, distancing himself from the device resting in Quinn's open hand, as though something would blow up in his face, right then and there. "Where the hell did you get that?"

"Don't worry about it."

"I never signed on for this. You've lost your mind! There's got to be a better way."

"Maybe. Maybe not." Quinn slipped the detonator back into his pocket.

What was Quinn thinking? The guy was out of his right mind. He'd lost all sense of sanity and connection to what really mattered. He clearly didn't care that he'd just gotten out of prison, since he was willing to risk his and everyone else's lives right now.

Tyler looked back at Max through the engineering room door's window.

Quinn didn't share or even acknowledge Tyler's concern. "It'll be over soon," he said. "We'll figure the rest out once we have the cash. For now, just watch my back."

A helicopter sounded overhead. The noise seemed to envelop the whole world, as the chopper moved to land on the helipad one story above them.

Quinn paused and looked to be in deep thought. "I think you might be right."

"Right about what?"

"About finding a better way." Quinn pushed Tyler aside and stepped back to the engineering room.

Tyler stood frozen in the open doorway, contemplating his options and finding none.

Quinn grabbed Akira Suzuki by the crook of her elbow with one swift motion. "I need to borrow our young guest for a moment."

Max stepped in between Quinn and the girl. "Leave her out of this."

"Too late for that." Quinn shoved his sister backward, and she fell against one of the control panels. "I'm just borrowing her for a minute."

Max steadied herself and looked as though she were about to pounce, but something in the look Quinn gave her stopped her dead in her tracks.

"I'm telling you not to worry about it, so don't. I have things handled." He lifted Akira by her waist. She tried to twist out of his grip, only to be met with a tighter grasp and the pinching sensation that came with struggling.

Akira's screams and cries were the only noise that could be heard over the sound of the chopper overhead.

"No!" Suzuki screamed, trying to jump out of his seat and run, then falling because of his bad leg. His cane was still against the wall on the other side of the room.

Tyler followed after Quinn. He looked back once to see Max restraining the desperate father.

The door closed behind him. He could still hear the anguished screams of Suzuki calling out for his daughter. It would haunt him just as Dibner's had.

# TWENTY

THE WETSUIT ALLOWED THE PENETRATING WATER TO WARM TO HER BODY'S temperature but she the initial injections sent the cold deep into her bones. Hatch held the left side of the Swim Buddy with her right hand and kept her left alongside her body, giving her a streamline. Cruise was close by on her right. Their bodies bumping every once in a while, serving as constant reminder she was not alone in the dark abyss they travelled through. The glow from the display's navigation system cast an eerie greenish yellow hue. Beyond that was an impenetrable wall of black.

Bubbles from the device's propellor system tickled their way across her face. Hatch moved her legs in a smooth flutter kick. She was grateful for the warmth generated from the exertion. Every thirty seconds or so Cruise would pass over the Draeger's mouthpiece. The oxygen staved off the burning in her muscles and reduced the subtle panic she felt rising up inside as they blindly moved beneath the surface of the ocean.

Hatch remembered the experience in the pool in Coronado. In open water, she felt the push and pull of the current. Out of her element, Cruise became the anchor of her calm.

Time seemed an elusive concept under the water. The only reference for the distance travelled came by way of the display. They crossed the fifteen-hundred-meter mark as a blip on the display came into view.

A strong current made the last five hundred meters the most challenging. Hatch's lungs began to burn, and she had begun switching out the mouthpiece more frequently. She tried to calm her mind and slow her breathing.

Cruise handed off the mouthpiece one last time and tapped Hatch on the shoulder. He then gestured with a thumbs up and pointed upward into the blackness.

Hatch felt Cruise tilt the Swim Buddy's yellow nose up at a forty-five-degree angle, and they began a steady ascent. In less than a minute, they broke the surface into the cold night air and were greeted by a steady rain. Hatch inhaled deeply; the fresh air never tasted so good.

They bobbed along the rough sea and looked up at the transfer station towering above. The four legs of the platform protruding up into the cloud covered sky above. Ahead, twenty feet away, was the dock. A small fishing boat was tethered alongside. No sign of Suzuki or his daughter. And no sign of Tyler and the Russell siblings. They floated, taking a moment to survey their objective. Satisfied the coast was clear, they made their final approach.

Hatch and Cruise came to a halt as they reached the transfer site's dock. Hatch disentangled herself from the Swim Buddy and grabbed onto the lowest rung of the ladder to climb up to the wooden platform. She laid on her stomach and surveyed the area. No sign of a threat. But she felt a liquid coat her right palm. It was too warm and thick to have been ocean water, or even rain. She couldn't see its color well due to the darkness around them.

She removed a Glock 23 subcompact from her waterproof pack and stood in a crouched position as her eyes traced over the dock and spotted the blood's point of origin, next to a wooden post closest to a stairwell leading up to the facility. By the way the blood had spread out, she could tell that whoever had been injured had not stumbled and oozed their way up the steps.

"Someone was injured here," Hatch said. "And whoever did it, dragged them up those steps."

Cruise finished putting the Swim Buddy in electronic tether mode to circle around the facility while they weren't using it. Then he climbed up the ladder and followed her visual observations, scanning the surface himself. "We better move then. Coming up." He laid on his stomach until Hatch gave him a nod, signaling 'all clear.'

He stood to the same crouch as Hatch and removed his gun from his pack.

They took off their flippers and moved at a low-ready in almost synchronous fashion.

Hatch stayed in front while Cruise followed her, staying low enough and moving in quiet steps so as not alert anyone of their presence.

They ascended the steps, following the trail of blood. Hatch heard Cruise slip behind her. The bottom steps were slick with sea spray and now blood. She halted and looked back, seeing the man regain his footing. He wiped his hand against his outer layer and readjusted the gun in his hand. Cruise threw her a nod to continue moving.

At the top of the steps, they reached a door into the facility. Hatch took up along the door's hinge side. She reached across with her left hand and gripped the handle. A slight turn confirmed the door was unlocked. Hatch looked at Cruise stacked opposite her. His weapon hovered at chest height with the nose pointed down. He gave a quick nod of his head.

Hatch yanked the handle down and shoved her shoulder against the door. Cruise's weapon came up as he entered. Hatch was tight on his heels. Cruise continued straight for a few steps. As soon as Hatch passed the door, she planted her foot, button-hooking and clearing the alternate enclosed hallway, following the trail of blood. Inside, the walkway continued in both directions. Hatch and Cruise each had a clear path. No target in sight.

Loud machinery enveloped her senses as they navigated through the building. No one would be able to hear them, but they wouldn't be able to hear anyone else either.

Going back down the hallway, Hatch noticed a room to her right labeled 'Engineering.' The trail of blood ended where the doorway began.

Hatch continued down the hallway and rounded the corner, just enough to not be spotted. She stuck her head out to see the engineering room door swing open in her peripheral vision as Cruise stayed at the opposite corner.

They heard the pained scream of Suzuki from somewhere inside just as two men stepped out and headed in the opposite direction with a small girl. Akira. She leaned in further to get a better look at the men, satisfied they probably wouldn't notice her. They were on a mission. She realized it was none other than Tyler Pierce and Quinn Russell, the latter holding a gun and the child. That wasn't a good combination. The trio left through a doorway labeled "Helipad Access."

"Divide and conquer?" Cruise asked in a whisper.

"Go with the known threat. We've got two of our three kidnappers on the move." She thought of Daphne and knew that if the shoe was on the other foot, saving the girl was priority one. Cruise didn't argue and took up beside her. With their weapons at the ready, they moved forward at a pace somewhere between a shuffle and a jog. Keeping a level shooting platform as they headed toward another helipad access stairwell.

As they moved through the corridor and closer to their next set of stairs, the thumping of the chopper drowned everything else out. They used the noise to mask their footfalls as they picked up the pace.

Just as they reached a roof access door opposite the one where Tyler and Quinn had taken Akira, the rotors of the helicopter began slowing to a stop. They had to be careful or whoever was up there would be able to hear Hatch and Cruise approaching.

Hatch began to climb the tall staircase, followed by Cruise. The whir of the helicopter's engine grew louder as they made their way up. She reached the top and crouched behind a pile of wooden boxes, hidden from sight of everyone on the helipad. At this angle, they wouldn't be able to see her or Cruise, but she could see them. She let go of one hand and made a "stop" signal to Cruise, letting him know she'd stay there at least a few minutes longer. He stayed directly behind her, leaning over slightly to get his own view of the scene in front of them.

She saw the disgruntled looking man in his thirties holding a rifle to the back of Akira Suzuki's little head. This must be Quinn Russell, Hatch thought. The prediction she'd made earlier that day was beginning to ring true. Quinn had a dirty objective, and would kill anyone—even innocent young girls—to achieve it.

The girl stood in front of Quinn, shaking with violent sobs. She stood as still as she could and barely made a noise as Quinn stayed behind her, unmoving, and ready to pull the trigger.

Hatch wanted to run to the girl, scoop her up, and take her away. But if she moved from her current position, she'd spook Quinn, and he'd pull the trigger, ending the life of Akira Suzuki.

Hatch stayed put, breathing deep and focusing on the scene in front of her until it was time to make a move.

The helicopter rotors came to their final stop, and the door swung open. Theo Clay stepped out as anticipated, followed by his security. The pilot stayed still in his seat. Parker Chase held a briefcase, the contents of which she could only assume were wads and wads of cash.

A ransom exchange.

At the same time, a young man stepped in from an access point directly across the helipad from Hatch's location. He approached Quinn to stand behind him. Hatch could read Tyler Pierce's expression immediately. Distraught, confused, numb.

Hatch could hear Clay's voice loud and clear. "There is no need to shoot the girl. I have everything you want in this briefcase."

Quinn's mouth drew up into a devious smile. "Consider her as an extra insurance policy."

Akira squealed. Hatch looked for a clear shot. Finding none, she stayed low and began working herself into a better advantage point.

"There's no need for all this. We had a deal." Clay's voice flashed with anger.

"Never make a deal with the devil unless you're willing to pay your dues." Quinn dropped the smile and met Clay's stare.

Hatch saw the conviction in Quinn's eyes and heard it in his voice. She'd seen it too many times before, and knew there was only one way this was going to end.

In the quiet that followed, Hatch prepared for a resolution of her own design.

## TWENTY-ONE

Rain poured onto the helipad and those standing on it. The surface was lit only by the emergency lights on the ground and the headlights from the helicopter. The chopper had come to a complete stop at this point. The wind blowing through Theo Clay's hair was that of natural forces, no longer the rotor blades. Parker Chase stood to the right of his boss, holding the briefcase.

Hatch stayed crouched behind a pile of boxes at the top of the stairs, hiding her position from the men on the helipad.

No opening yet. She was waiting for the right time to jump in and make her move.

Quinn hardened his expression. He wrapped his right arm around the young girl in front of him and crouched lower, using her as a human shield. The assault rifle was slung around his right shoulder. Pointing to the back of her head was a small pistol he'd grabbed from the back of his waistband. Turning to look at Tyler, his expression remained steady, and he nodded at the other man.

Tyler strode in front of them, moving closer to Clay and Chase.

"Which of you is Quinn?" Clay asked.

"I'm supposed to get the money from you," Tyler said.

"And are you Quinn?"

"It doesn't matter."

Hatch watched the exchange and listened the best she could through the pouring rain. Just moments ago, the young man had seemed so distraught with his involvement. She'd seen the frightened look on his face earlier too, when she'd come so close to shooting him. If Tyler made one small misstep, Hatch would have no choice but to end the young man's life. If he was in too deep, he would have a hefty price to pay. Would she be willing to end his life to save the others, when she hadn't been earlier today?

She looked back at Cruise. "What do we do?" she whispered.

Cruise shrugged and glanced back at the helipad. "Seems like he's in all the way. You sure you're up for this?"

Hatch looked back at the scene. "I have to be."

"That wasn't the arrangement," Clay said, walking toward Tyler. "I was supposed to hand the money over to Quinn in exchange for my colleague and his daughter. And here you have her at gunpoint. That was not the arrangement." He stood about a foot in front of Tyler now.

Hatch could tell Tyler was nervous by the way he swallowed every few seconds and held his hands clenched into tight fists. His chest began to move in and out in a faster rhythm, signifying his uptick in adrenaline and oxygen intake.

From behind him, Hatch noticed Parker Chase hold the briefcase higher than before. He took a gun out of a pocket inside his jacket and raised it behind the briefcase, hiding it from their adversaries. But not from Hatch.

She didn't let this turn of events sway her from the task at hand. Hatch kept her aim on Quinn, avoiding the girl and waiting for the right shot.

"This is getting out of hand." Clay took a step back from Tyler, looking disgusted and regrouping.

Quinn loosened his grip around the girl's shoulders as he moved toward the briefcase.

Hatch looked down at Cruise. "Hey, I think I can make this shot."

"Don't miss."

"I never miss."

Hatch pointed her gun around the boxes at Quinn's leg. The goal was not to kill the man, but rather knock him off balance and deter his way forward—physically, and metaphorically.

Chase tossed the briefcase at Quinn, and Akira slipped out from under his grasp. Chase now had his gun revealed and aimed it at Quinn.

Hatch still kept her aim on Quinn, too.

Before Akira could bolt down the opposite stairwell, Quinn moved back to the girl, shoving Tyler out of the way and grabbing her shoulders, making her a human shield again.

Clay looked at Quinn, then back to Chase. Just over the rain, Hatch heard him mutter, "Kill him."

Chase didn't hesitate to shoot. The gunshot rang out, hitting Quinn, and narrowly missing Akira. The bullet landed squarely on Quinn's chest. Akira broke free again, this time heading straight for the stairwell. Tyler caught her and restrained her by an arm.

Over the sound of the rain, Hatch heard the helicopter rotors restart their loud churn. Clay raced to the aircraft from the middle of the helipad, leaving Chase to follow in his wake. A burst of machine gunfire sprayed at the chopper, hitting the side just above Clay. He dove to the slippery concrete ground and covered his head, as though his bare hands could protect him from that level of fire.

Quinn got back to his feet, bleeding profusely from his chest. He held the rifle in his right hand, steadied against the front of his right shoulder. Fire exploded from the gun again. Chase dove to avoid getting hit by it. The bullets hit the windshield and the pilot behind it, killing him instantly. The rotors slowed again.

Quinn had moved back toward the door he'd come through, close to the other stairwell. Tyler stood behind him, no longer grasping Akira, but keeping her behind him to protect her.

Chase laid on his stomach as he fired at Quinn again, missing, hitting the door frame behind the other man. Chase kept firing until his trigger made a light clicking noise.

Quinn had avoided every shot Chase attempted. All except that first one. He was still bleeding from his chest, and his skin was losing color. Tyler pulled Akira into the stairwell to keep her safe.

Quinn looked at Clay and Chase and stretched his mouth in a blood-coated smile. He pulled a small remote out of his back pocket.

A bomb detonator.

The rain fell harder as Quinn pressed the small red button.

A loud explosion sounded from underneath them as the structure began to crackle and pop. The helipad split in half and collapsed at the unsupported corner. Quinn rushed into the stairwell, following Tyler and Akira, just as the helicopter slid from its place on the skid pad and blocked the opposite doorway.

The slick concrete beneath her feet jutted upward, tossing Hatch into the air. She landed on her back, the impact knocking the wind out of her. The momentum of her fall coupled with the wet surface sent Hatch hurtling headfirst into the metal corner of the stairwell access. Searing pain shot from her skull down her spine. Bright flashes dotted her vision, and she fought against the encroaching darkness, willing herself to remain conscious.

Hatch reached up and felt the gash on the top of her head. Her hand was slick with blood. She pressed herself against the doorframe. Using it as a crutch, she brought herself to a standing position. The wooziness subsided, and she took two deep combat breaths and got herself back in the fight.

Cruise gave her a look of concern.

"I'm good to go." Hatch wiped at the trail of blood stinging her eye. The platform groaned. "We need to get those hostages and get the hell off this thing! Not sure how long it's going to hold."

Hatch moved to the stairwell. Her legs wobbled. She returned her gun to the small of her back so she could use both hands on the railing to navigate her way down.

Cruise led the way. The stairs had shifted in the partial collapse. Hatch felt as though she was inside M.C. Escher's Relativity drawing of the ascending/descending staircase.

Three steps down and Hatch lost her footing, almost kicking Cruise in the back of his head. He helped her steady herself.

"That cut on your head—"

"Nothing a couple stiches and stiff drink can't fix. We've got bigger fish to fry."

Cruise got the message and pressed no further. He descended the remaining steps in a matter of seconds and Hatch was tight on his tail.

They ran along the edge of the platform. Each step pounded in her head like a jackhammer.

Cruise blasted through the door into the platform's interior.

Hatch followed him into the hallway. The lights above flickered, creating a strobe effect. They paused for a moment, scanning their surroundings. Hatch retrieved her pistol and held it at a low ready.

Steel support beams screamed out as the destabilized helipad folded. "Move!" Hatch yelled.

Her words were cut off as the ceiling above collapsed, raining concrete down on them. The last thing Hatch saw before the flickering world around her faded to black was the ton of debris falling, and Cruise collapsing beneath it.

## TWENTY-TWO

"No!" Suzuki sobbed as Quinn took away his only daughter. He didn't want to begin imagining what the man could do with the assault rifle held in his other hand. "How could you let this happen?" Looking over at the female captor, she didn't bat an eye or even flinch at the sound of his voice. Her face was made of stone, though he couldn't see it well due to the dim red lighting in the room.

Suzuki sighed and bowed his head. "That guy's still losing a lot of blood." Nodding toward the unconscious guard on the floor at the side of the room. Dark blood saturated the thin fabric wrapped around the wound. Soon it would seep out as if the fabric hadn't been there at all.

"I did what I could," the girl said.

"Listen, Max? Is it okay if I call you that?" Suzuki had been in the business world long enough and understood the value of using first names. The same tactic utilized by hostage negotiators. Humanize and it becomes difficult to execute.

Nodding, she said nothing.

"You don't want his death on your hands. Trust me."

She avoided eye contact with Suzuki.

"I can help you. If you just let me—"

"Just stay where you are. I can manage." Her voice held little confidence.

"Look, I'm no threat to you. You have my cane and I can't get away. Plus, you're armed." He nodded at the gun held in her right hand. "You need to apply pressure to the man's wound or let me. Otherwise, he will bleed out."

Finally she looked over at Suzuki. Compassion flashed across her face for a split second, taken over by contemplation as she weighed the risks of letting him free.

"Turn your head away," she said. Suzuki complied. Hearing the sound of footsteps, he then felt the sharp edge of a knife find its way into the binds around his wrists. They'd tied him to the seat as an extra precaution.

He slid down from his seat to the floor, then scooted himself over to the guard.

"Do you have any water?"

The girl moved from her crossed-armed position and rummaged through a duffle bag. Taking out a bottle of water, she tossed it to Suzuki.

Opening the cap, he parted the guard's lips with his thumb. Then he tipped the bottle into his mouth. The man coughed as he let the water dribble out of his mouth. Suzuki kept pouring and gently telling him to swallow and take small sips. He eventually became conscious enough to snatch the bottle from Suzuki's hand and sip on his own. Suzuki used this time to apply pressure on the wound and noticed the guard's putrid odor. Maybe from his wound, or possibly his long shift.

"What's the cane for, anyway?" The girl asked. She now sat on one of the chairs and had her legs pulled up to her chest. With her arms wrapped around her knees as if giving herself a hug.

Suzuki was both shocked and relieved by the question. He hadn't expected the girl would make small talk. Then again, she didn't read like the type to be involved in a kidnapping either.

He continued applying pressure to the man's leg as he looked up at the girl. He didn't like to tell the story, but what did he have to lose? "It seems like forever now. When I was a young man, about the same age as your friend. Having studied Kyokushin Karate for the better part of my life, I had been training for the regional championship. A big honor where I'm from. Like your Super Bowl. My sparring partner and best friend had helped me prepare. I've always been a quick learner, and the better I got, the more he distanced himself from me. Resented me. Well, I ended up winning the title with a round kick. It was my strongest technique. Fast and deadly accurate. The kick landed on my opponent's neck, knocking him unconscious.

"After the fight, I walked through an alley on my way home. Someone in a hoodie came up to me and smashed my leg with a lead pipe. It shattered my knee and made it so I couldn't fight again after that." Gesturing to the girl for more gauze, she handed it to him and he continued wrapping it tightly around the injured leg. "I looked into my assaulter's eyes after I hit the ground. Even though the shadows shrouded his features, I could still see. The man in the hoodie was my long-time sparring partner. That day, I learned about the cost of victory and how those closest can turn against you."

Max slowly nodded her head, letting his words hang in the air.

Suzuki stared down at the man's leg as he continued to wrap it. He just shook his head.

"Have you ever told your daughter that story?"

Shaking his head again, this time he looked back into the girl's eyes.

"Why not?"

"You ask a lot of questions."

"Can you blame me for being curious about the people we kidnapped?"

The corner of Suzuki's mouth quirked into a half-smile. "I never taught her to fight or told her that story because I wanted to protect her. There are too many horrors in this world, and I thought I could safeguard her innocence. Apparently, I miscalculated." His stare bore deep into the woman across from him.

She looked down at her knees, then planted her feet on the floor. "I am really sorry about all this. Like Tyler said earlier, this was never part of the plan. I had no idea we were going to kidnap you, but when Quinn told us we had to in order to get the money, I didn't feel like I had a choice. Look, I don't expect you to forgive me, but can you understand why I did it?"

"Yes, I understand," Suzuki said. "But you seem like a good person. Can you understand that I expect you to make this right?"

The girl gave an almost imperceptible nod.

Suzuki shifted his tone. "You need to watch out for your brother. He's becoming more and more unhinged. I know he's the one behind all of this. You can still do the right thing."

"You're right." Reaching beside her, she threw Suzuki his cane.

"Go find your daughter," she said. "I'll look after the guard."

Suzuki held onto his cane, stunned at the girl's gesture.

"This is how I make it right," she said.

As Suzuki pressed down on his cane to get to his feet, a loud explosion sounded beneath them. The floor shifted, crashing Suzuki back to the ground. The red glow of the control panel lights vanished as the room fell into darkness.

## TWENTY-THREE

Hatch stirred, finding herself under a pile of debris and lead piping. She would've been rendered unconscious if not for the adrenaline pumping through her veins. That and the thick piece of rebar acting as an archway.

Crawling forward, she clawed her way over the debris field. Darkness surrounded her like the water they'd navigated to get here. Only difference now was that Cruise was no longer at her side.

Blindly inching forward, Hatch's body was firing off alerts to the damage she'd sustained in the collapse. Nothing broken, but bruises and lacerations lined her extremities. The scar along her right arm had fresh damage. Scars upon scars. It would be another memory etched deep into the tapestry of her flesh. No time to lick wounds and count blessings. The only good thing to come from the intense pain radiating throughout her body was she no longer paid notice to the throbbing in her head.

Hatch focused on one thing, and one thing only. Finding Cruise.

"Cruise?" she called out, her words choked by a thick cloud of concrete dust floating in the air. No answer. "I'm coming for you! Listen to the sound of my voice."

She shoved the pile of weight off her with a forceful grunt and scanned the area.

*Shit.*

Freeing her legs from the tunnel, she moved into a low crouch. A red emergency light flickered above the stairwell access they'd just exited. The door completely sealed by a chunk of concrete the size of a recliner. Beside it was a heap of twisted black that stood out amidst the beige cement. It took a second for her eyes to adjust to what she was looking at.

Cruise was facedown, his lean body a crumpled heap. A piece of the ceiling had collapsed on top of him. The Draeger served as a barrier between the rubble and him. He lay motionless. In the poorly lit conditions, Hatch couldn't see the rise and fall of his chest. She choked back the dark thoughts creeping into her mind.

In the passing millisecond upon seeing him, Hatch's mind was flooded with regret. What had she been thinking, leaving their relationship at that kind of standstill, not opening up to him, not telling him how she felt? Why did she keep him at arm's length? What hold did Savage have on her? She thought of all the things not said.

Then she heard a groan.

She sprinted down the pile of rubble, though careful not to trip and fall again. When she reached him, she dug through everything that had fallen on him and pulled him out, repositioning him to face her and lay his head on her lap. Moaning again, he coughed, moving the mouthpiece out of the way. The Draeger's acted as a barrier between Cruise and the fallen debris. In the process, the Draeger had been crushed under collapsed structure and was now inoperable.

That might be a problem for the future, but they would worry about that later. She breathed a sigh of relief as his eyes fluttered open in a dry squint. The waves in her mind rested as her heartbeat settled. She still had time to make things right with him.

His cheeks and hands were bruised. No doubt more of his body would have been too, but they would tend to it later.

"Are you hurt?" Hatch asked him. "Anything broken?"

Cruise sat up and knocked the debris off his body. "A little banged up, but I'll take a couple bruises over a broken leg any day." He smiled at her. She felt a surge of warmth spread through her chest.

"Your head." He grazed a finger across the dried blood on her scalp. "We should take care of that soon."

"I can't even feel it," Hatch responded. "Are you really sure you want to say goodbye to all of this?"

Cruise chuckled softly.

"A lot less bumps and bruises in the restaurant business. What's the fun in that?"

Cruise continued to grin as he sat himself up and brushed the dust off.

Hatch stood and offered her hands to help him to his feet.

There was no way through the hallway where they were to the engineering room. It was sealed off a few feet from the door, which also meant no access to the dock from their position. Hatch looked at the access door to the stairwell they'd just descended before the collapse. A large boulder stood in their way. Hatch fished out a long piece of rebar. "Worth a shot."

Hatch jammed the steel rod underneath. She and Cruise leaned hard into the rod. The rock shifted a couple of inches, but not enough to grant them access. Hatch cursed under her breath. "We need a fulcrum to give us leverage."

Cruise searched the ground for something to wedge in place. He was down on all fours when Hatch saw it. Actually, Cruise was wearing it. "The Draeger's wrecked. It should fit."

Cruise undid the straps and set it at the base of the rebar. After several minutes of intense struggling, the boulder moved enough for them to gain access to the door. But the platform's shifting had jammed the door.

Hatch slammed her shoulder into the hard steel, sending a ripple of pain down her shoulder. Taking turns, they used their bodies as battering rams until the door gave way. Squeezing through the tight opening, they entered the stairwell and headed back up to the fractured helipad.

They reached the top of the stairwell and the helipad access door. Rain splashed on them and the frequent gusts of wind almost sent them tumbling back down. It took both of them pulling the door handle to get it open against the howling wind.

The stairwell to the helipad was tilted inward, but the pipes and debris had stopped falling at this point. They had to use their hands and feet again in a sort of monkey climb to get over everything and closer to the helipad.

On the other side of the stairwell, where Hatch had lined up her shot on Quinn Russell, the chopper had slid toward the other helipad access door. The helipad itself was capsized at a slant, sure to tumble at any moment. The unsupported half that had fallen off earlier was long gone in the ocean by now.

Stepping onto the helipad with their guns at the ready, they saw no one. It was eerily quiet. Had no one survived the wreck, or had they all escaped?

They passed by the fallen helicopter and the dead pilot inside. Checking the windows, there was no sign of Theo Clay or Parker Chase. They leaned over the side of the helipad, searching for survivors in the water. No one.

They exchanged glances and began sprinting back across the helipad, to the other stairwell access. The same route Quinn and Tyler had used. The blockage from before was gone. The secondary collapse must've helped to clear the path.

They maneuvered past the helicopter, precariously balanced atop the raised split in the helipad. Its nose pointed down, teetering in the wind like a ski jumper preparing for launch.

Hatch took the lead as they entered the stairwell. A gust of wind slammed the door closed, sealing them in darkness as they descended in search of Akira and the others.

## TWENTY-FOUR

Tyler walked behind Akira down the corridor, protecting her from Quinn, who was following closely behind him. Quinn was bleeding profusely from his skull. A pipe had fallen and hit him hard in the head after the explosion. His chest continued to ooze red, and he coughed up blood every five seconds as he fought to catch up to Tyler. Part of the structure had fallen on top of him earlier, but he still held onto the assault rifle in his hand and the detonator in the other. He'd tucked the handgun into the back of his waistband.

Quinn spat blood in Tyler's direction. "Wait up."

Tyler looked back and saw Quinn using the machine gun as a cane. His blood dripped on the floor, leaving a thin trail behind them. Tyler didn't acknowledge the other man. Turning back around, he leaned down to whisper to Akira. "When I move, I want you to run as fast as you can around that corner."

Quinn's voice sounded behind Tyler again, louder this time, echoing through the hall. "If you don't get back here and help me, I won't hesitate to put a bullet through your skull."

Tyler stopped in his tracks. "Run."

Akira sprinted down the hall, her long dark hair flowing behind her.

Quinn hobbled to Tyler, trying to lift the gun to point at the girl, then he laughed, showing his bloody teeth. "There goes the leverage."

Tyler stood in front of Akira's position, blocking the other man from taking aim at the young girl. "Don't talk about her that way. She's a kid, dude. And you tried to exchange her for ransom."

Quinn lowered the gun to the ground and leaned his weight on it. "I know. I never thought it would go this far."

Tyler was surprised to hear the words from the other man's mouth. He couldn't hide it. "Taking people hostage and detonating bombs. Shooting an innocent man on the job, who had nothing to do with any of this, for heaven's sake. At what point did you realize you'd gone too far?"

Quinn sighed. "A million dollars was what Max and I needed. We need it to pay for our mom's treatment. Plus, there would have been extra to donate to causes and even a little left for you." His speech was slurring from the blood loss. The look of innocence and remorse was torn back down by his ever-present defiance. "You're gonna get me and Max off this rig, or nobody leaves."

Tyler shook his head. For a moment there, he'd pitied the guy. He turned away from Quinn and continued walking down the hallway, following the path Akira had taken.

Quinn called after him. "They were never gonna let us live, anyway. You think someone would be so stupid as to give us a million dollars flat?" Quinn nudged Tyler in the back with his rifle.

Tyler's chest swelled with rage. He turned back around in time to swat the rifle out of his way. "Enough."

"Don't think I won't kill you." Quinn's face was now mere inches from Tyler's. "Just because my sister's got a little crush on you don't make your life worth saving."

Max did reciprocate Tyler's feelings! What a time to find out.

As inconvenient as the timing was, Tyler still felt a surge of power and confidence rush through his body. "Try me."

The ex-con lunged at Tyler. Quinn brought the weapon up. His injuries made his movements slow. Tyler seized the advantage, grabbing the end of the long barrel. He tugged down hard, wrenching Quinn's shoulder and pulling him forward.

A rage filled inside him as he thought of all Quinn had put him through over the last couple days. He thought about Dibner, about Akira, and then Max. Tyler closed his fist, his knuckles white. He swung his fist like a wrecking ball, raining down blow after blow. He felt Quinn's nose shatter with a sickening sound. Blood gushed, coating his tormentor in a goatee of red molasses.

Quinn howled and staggered back. The muzzle slipped from Tyler's grasp. Quinn was deranged, his eyes burned with murderous intent. There was no doubt in Tyler's mind. Quinn Russell planned to kill him, right here, right now.

Tyler had no time to grab the pistol tucked in the back of his waistband. Quinn was already drawing the weapon upward, taking aim at Tyler's chest.

Tyler lunged. This time, instead of trying to grab the end of the barrel, he opted for an all-out tackle. Tyler wrapped Quinn in a bearhug, effectively pinning the assault rifle between them.

A deafening bang reverberated through Tyler's body. Like two magnets of opposite polarity, both men sprang apart. He looked down at his blood covered hands. Tyler couldn't breathe. Panic racked his mind. His hands frantically searching his body for the gunshot wound. It took a moment for his brain to catch up and realize the blood wasn't his.

Quinn stood motionless. The rage of a moment ago was replaced by something else, something Tyler had never seen in Max's older brother. Fear.

The gun drooped down by Quinn's side. He swayed for what seemed like an eternity before collapsing to the floor. Tyler, still not convinced the threat was over, dove on top.

Tyler pinned him down at the shoulders. Blood continued to gurgle out of Quinn's mouth and nose, draining from his skull in spurts. Tyler released his grip on the man.

Quinn coughed, words mixing with blood. Tyler leaned in close enough to hear.

"Tell Max I'm sorry." Each word coming at great cost.

Tyler released his hold and sank to the ground next to him. The bullet hole pumping blood from Quinn's chest with each beat of his heart.

"You gotta get my sister off this thing." His eyelids fluttered. "It's going to blow."

"What do you mean?" Tyler trying to make sense of the dying man's mumblings. "There's another bomb?"

"We leave or nobody does." The words dripped from his mouth like a leaky faucet.

"Where's the detonator?"

Quinn shook his head. His body convulsed violently. "Timer."

"How long?"

Quinn could no longer speak. He only managed enough strength to tap the watch on his wrist. Tyler grabbed it, wiping clear the blood smear until the digital face became clear enough to read.

Quinn let out a long slow rattle and then he was gone. *Another bomb?*

Tyler removed the watch from Quinn's wrist and stuck it in his pocket. He took a couple of precious seconds to take the rifle from Quinn's lifeless hand.

Tyler stumbled back to his feet, regaining what composure he could muster and then broke into a run. Away from the man he'd just murdered. Toward the girl he was trying to protect.

He rounded the corner and found Akira shaking in a little ball on the floor.

"I heard a loud popping noise from down the hall," she said. Then she looked up at him. She eyed him up and down, processing all the bright blood on his clothes. Her eyes went wide with fear when she saw the gun in his hand. Tyler wasn't sure why he'd grabbed it in the first place. Without a second thought, he threw the gun into the water and the girl relaxed.

"It's over now. He won't hurt you," Tyler said. "Now let's go find your father. We don't have much time."

He wiped the palms of his hands on his pants. Taking the young girl's hand in his, the two made off down the corridor toward the engineering room. Tyler hoped the blast didn't kill Max. And hoping if it didn't, that she'd ever find it in her heart to forgive him for what he'd just done.

None of it would matter if they didn't find a way off this platform, and fast. The clock was ticking. He felt each passing second in the thrumming of his rapidly beating heart.

## TWENTY-FIVE

The explosion had tossed Max to the other side of the room. Her world had gone dark. For a second, she thought she'd been rendered unconscious. To her disappointment, she was still awake and alive. The power had just gone out.

Still recovering from the force and impact of landing on the floor, she crawled with her elbows and legs, searching for Suzuki. In the darkness, she couldn't see where he had landed. She was closer to the side of the room. Her hand brushed against the door handle. Max continued to move along the wall with her hand gliding against it. Then she moved her hand to the floor, feeling her way around the room. Her palm found a puddle of warm, thick liquid. She felt her way across the wet floor. She held her hands to her face. It took her a moment to recognize the scent. The wetness around her wasn't water, she'd found herself in a puddle of blood left by the wounded guard.

Max found the wound with her bloodied hand, then skimmed over him to his arm, down to his wrist to feel his pulse. Weak, but there. And he was still upright.

Groans filled the silence. "Suzuki?"

He responded with another groan.

"I'll be right there," she promised.

Keeping her attention on the guard for the moment she felt around the floor checking for any loose bandage that might have fallen from his leg. She tightened it back around his thigh. Then she found a pipe on the floor next to her and cranked it on the injury to set a tourniquet. The bleeding slowed immediately.

"Thank you," the weak guard murmured through his gag.

Max wiped her palm on her pants and didn't waste any time getting back to her search for Suzuki. He still groaned from the middle of the room. He must have collapsed right where he stood. Max continued to crawl on her elbows and knees. She landed on his cane, so he couldn't have gone far. A few more feet, and her elbow had reached the man's ankle.

"My leg," Suzuki called. His voice sounded weak, withered. "It's trapped."

Max got to her knees and stuck her hands out in front of her. They landed on a steel table that had been upright before. She couldn't tell how his leg was bent underneath, how it had gotten trapped in the first place.

She was working at trying to lift a table leg when the backup generator kicked on. The light provided was minimal compared to what they'd had earlier, but it was enough to see what she was doing and where Suzuki's bad leg had gotten stuck.

Max got to her feet and lifted the table from the bottom, allowing Suzuki to pull his leg away. Letting the table fall back where it had landed, she grabbed Suzuki's cane.

She slumped against the wall next to Suzuki and sighed. This was the first moment of peace she'd found the whole night.

But it wouldn't last.

Gunshots sounded from the outer hall. Max could tell it wasn't directly next to them, but it might as well have been.

What felt like seconds later, banging sounded from the door. Max felt her adrenaline rise again as she got to her feet to open it. She gripped her gun, ready to fire at any moment. But when she opened the door, in front of her stood a mussed-haired Tyler with Akira behind him.

"Where is my daughter?" Yohei Suzuki called. He sat next to the guard on the floor.

Akira poked her head out from behind Tyler. The girl forced Max out of the way as she found her father and ran to embrace him. Tyler was now directly in front of Max.

"Where's Quinn?" she asked.

Tyler shook his head. His mouth moved as if he wanted to say something, but he couldn't get the words to come out.

Max's eyes trailed over Tyler's bloody appearance, and she stumbled back.

Her breathing became fast and shallow as she gripped the counter behind her. Her brother had died. Tyler couldn't have killed him, could he have?

Then she looked back at Tyler. "What happened back there? Did Quinn detonate the bomb?"

"Yeah."

"Is that what killed him?"

"No."

"So that second noise. Was that—"

"Yeah."

Tyler looked down. She could see the guilty look in his eyes. He hadn't meant to shoot the other man. He could explain later. Max nodded in understanding.

Her breathing slowed. Part of her was relieved her brother was gone. Another part of her was guilty for being relieved. But Quinn had really lost his mind. Max cared about her mother and wanted the money as bad as he did, but Tyler was right. Max could find a job and take care of her mother over time. It probably wouldn't be the best job, but minimum wage was better than nothing at all. And it was definitely better than stealing.

Good or bad, Quinn was her brother. The loss still filled her soul and made her heart ache. But she couldn't figure out what she felt. Anger, resentment, relief, sadness, remorse. And she couldn't figure out whether to cry or scream or shut down.

Usually, she tended toward the latter.

"I know you must be experiencing a lot right now," Tyler said, snapping Max out of her thoughts. Resting a hand on her shoulder, he looked in her eyes. "But we need to get out of here. We've got a bigger problem to deal with." He moved to the guard and began untying the man and removing the gag from his mouth. "That wasn't the only bomb."

Max's eyes went wide with fear.

Suzuki got to his feet with Akira still clinging to his shirt. As the five began to make their way to the door, Theo Clay stood in front of the doorway, blocking their exit.

He stepped into the room and to the side of the door to reveal Parker Chase holding a gun and slowly changing his target back and forth between the five. Max raised her own handgun in response.

"Whoa, there's no need for this. It's over," Tyler said.

"You heard the boy," Clay said to Max. "It's over. Drop the gun."

Max didn't budge.

Tyler stepped in front of her, blocking her from Chase's aim. "We don't even have your money, man. We're nothing to you."

Chase moved to snatch Akira from her father before Suzuki could react. He held her as a shield in front of him and pointed the gun at her skull. "He said, drop the gun." Chase was unreadable in the dim lighting.

The young girl whimpered.

Max complied, tossing it to the floor, and Chase shoved the girl back into the room. Akira landed next to her father again. Balancing one hand on his cane, the other arm surrounded his daughter. She buried her face in his side.

"Quinn's dead, man. We don't have a deal anymore." Tyler looked at Theo Clay and crossed his arms in front of his chest.

Clay let out a cold, hard laugh. "Yes, I did see your handiwork with that. Thanks for your help, by the way." He moved into the room. Parker Chase planted himself in the doorframe.

Max took in a sharp breath. Tyler had been gentle about her brother's death. But the rich man in front of her ripped at the fact like a light-hearted joke.

"A little earlier than expected," Clay continued, "but a gift, nonetheless. I'm sure you two will have plenty to talk about later." He looked between Tyler and Max. "Now how about you all work yourselves back into those bindings?"

Tyler stood his ground. "There's another bomb! If we don't get off this godforsaken death trap in the next fifteen minutes, we're all dead. You hear me?"

Clay exchanged a look with Chase, who was keeping everyone at bay with the pistol in his hand. His eyes bore into Tyler's. "Tie them up."

Tyler began searching for all the bindings that had been undone over the course of the night.

"You'll start," Clay said, "with my wonderful partner. Yohei Suzuki."

Theo Clay held Max at gunpoint until the very moment Tyler finished binding everyone.

Tyler feigned tying Suzuki's bindings around his wrists, leaving them loose enough, so he could move freely when the time dictated. Tyler had leaned in to whisper to the older man. "I need a distraction. Be ready to move on my signal."

Suzuki gave Tyler a puzzled look. Tyler nodded to the cane only a few feet away before moving on to bind everyone else.

Tyler stood behind Max. "Be ready to move."

Max didn't move in acknowledgment. Didn't want to give away any planning to Clay or Chase.

Clay looked at Max as he clasped his hands in front of him. He wore a condescending smile. Tyler cringed at the older man's nonchalance. "Your screw-up brother did one thing right." He let the words soak in as Max winced at the memory of her now-deceased older brother. "We'd planned on just shooting you all. But a bomb blast would make this thing a lot less messy." Clay looked pleased with himself.

Tyler shook his head. "There's no time."

"For the rest of you. No. I'm afraid the sands in your hourglass have run out." Clay seemed to be enjoying himself. "How do you think she'll feel about you after she learns that you're the one who killed her brother? Maybe you won't have to wait for the next explosion? Maybe she'll do you in beforehand."

Tyler looked at Max with pleading eyes. "No, that's not what happened at all. I knocked the detonator away from him, and then he tried to point the rifle at me. I went to knock that away too, and it went off while pointing at him. I'm so sorry, Max, but I didn't shoot him. At least, I didn't mean for that to happen."

Max looked away from Tyler. He could feel the pain emanating from her.

"Aw, boo-hoo." Clay sauntered over to Max, mocking the young girl. She craned her neck to get her face away from the older man's, looking almost as though she'd snap her head off.

"You'll never get away with this," Suzuki said.

Clay laughed in defiance. He held his arms out to gesture to the world. "Oh, my dear friend, I already have gotten away with it. That one million in cash"—he lifted his fingers in air quotes and took on a mocking tone —"was only a small fraction of what I've taken from you."

Tyler and Max glanced over at Suzuki. Shock and desperation clashed on his face as he assessed the man in front of him. Presumably the person he thought he'd known so well. The monster that had allowed him to be kidnapped and held hostage.

Clay stepped toward Suzuki and narrowed his eyes at the other man. "The hundred-million-dollar transfer will go through first thing tomorrow morning, and there is nothing you can do to stop it."

Suzuki shook his head. His expression held disappointment and sorrow. "How could you turn on me, Theo?" He asked in a whisper.

Clay scoffed. "Me?" He held a hand to his chest in mock offense, then looked away and paced back and forth in front of the line of hostages. "I was there for you when you went into a catatonic state after your wife's death and almost let the company collapse into ruin." Clay raised his voice. "I was there to pick it up. I brokered this deal. I saw the future. You just sat there and cried like a child." Suzuki's expression personified disgust. Clay chuckled and continued his pacing. "But to make matters worse, you named your daughter as heir to the throne, to be the head of a company she doesn't even understand."

Max looked over at Suzuki, and Suzuki returned the glance. They seemed to come to a silent understanding when Suzuki turned his head to look back at his corrupt partner. Max then poked Akira with her foot and silently suggested the girl lean against the wall and give her father some space.

"I figured a hundred million dollars was severance pay and seemed fair enough."

Tyler picked up the cane without the other men noticing. Max stepped forward a hair to allow Tyler to slide the cane behind his back and behind hers, holding on to its end so Suzuki could grip onto the handle with his hands behind his back. Suzuki reoriented the cane until the bottom touched the floor.

"Plus, you do remember our contract, don't you?" Clay turned to face the group and approached Suzuki. "If you and your heir become deceased for any reason," Clay continued, "then the company goes to me." He wore a wild grin. Tyler saw him as something akin to the Joker. His face was just mere inches from Suzuki's now. Tyler could see the spittle landing on Suzuki's cheeks, even from a few feet away.

Suzuki balanced himself on the cane behind his legs so Clay couldn't see.

Clay took on a mock sympathizing face. "You always were weak and malleable, wouldn't you say?"

At that, Suzuki firmly planted the cane with his hands and lifted his good leg to slam a kick to the side of Clay's neck.

Clay collapsed onto the floor, howling in pain. The painful howls turned to growling as he rolled over onto his stomach and began crawling toward the door.

Tyler seized his window of opportunity and pulled the gun from the small of his back. Max swooped in and pulled Suzuki and Akira out of the line of fire as Tyler squeezed the trigger of the pistol in his hand.

The shots were wild. Tyler dove as Chase returned fire. A bullet zipped by his head striking a pipe. Steam sprayed into the room, providing concealment as they took cover behind the thick metal of the control station console.

Chase rushed toward Clay and hoisted him off the ground. "Time to go. They sealed their fate."

"The helicopter isn't an option, but they left us a boat."

"I'll be sure to say some truly moving words at your eulogy," Clay said as he followed Chase out the door.

"They're taking our boat!" Max hissed. "There's no way off this damn thing unless one of you know how to fly a chopper."

Silence. Tyler racked his brain for another option and came up empty handed.

"There's another. It's how we get to and from the mainland." The guard's voice was barely audible. "That is, if it's still there."

## TWENTY-SIX

Hatch and Cruise made their way down the open-air corridor in the dead of night. A backup generator had kicked the overhead lights back on. Rain rushed down into the ocean, missing them on the covered platform.

The pair tread carefully across the slanted platform to get to the other exit and down its hall. They could barely see the floor past the wreckage. Pipes had burst overhead or fallen to the ground. They had to climb with both their hands and legs over piles of debris to get down the hallway.

Just a few more feet in, the wreckage had piled and blocked the walkway from floor to ceiling.

"There's no way we're getting through that," Cruise said.

Hatch leaned over the side of the walkway. "We can climb around to the other side. It's just a few feet."

She unzipped the wetsuit and stuck her gun inside. Hatch tugged the zipper back up, tightening the weapon against her chest. She lowered herself to the ground, stabilizing her hands on the edge of the slick surface. Her hands were calloused and rough enough to maintain a decent grip. Carefully, she hooked one thumb under the side of the platform and kept the rest of her fingers on the walkway. Then she lowered her legs, keeping her other hand on the platform. When her legs were fully suspended in the air, she began to sidle from her current position, heading to the other end, past the obstacle.

Cruise followed close behind. "If this is how you go out, you're not going out alone."

"Why would this be how I go out?"

They began to breathe heavily, talking between pants as they inched their hands across the walkway like grabbing onto sideways monkey bars. "This walkway is super slick from all the rain and sea spray," Cruise said. "One wrong move, and we could be plummeting to the ocean."

Just then, Hatch's right hand lost its grip. She clenched her left hand to the platform, catching her breath. She turned to look at Cruise, who met her with a pointed look. "This is not how I go out," she said.

They made it to the other side of the wall of debris. They pulled themselves up with the strength of their arms, hitching one leg up and then the other. Cruise stopped in his tracks as he looked at the ground in front of them. "What?" Hatch asked, then followed his gaze and spotted him.

Quinn Russell lay on the ground in a pool of his own blood.

Hatch knelt to assess the damage to the man who couldn't have been any older than her. "There's the wound in his chest from Chase. Looks like a bullet to the base of his chin sent him out. Explains the last gunshot we heard."

Cruise nodded in agreement.

"He's also got some damage to his skull, probably from everything that fell from the explosion."

"What do we do?" Cruise asked.

"We can't take him with us," Hatch said. "He bled out, and now he's dead. We have to keep going to find everyone else."

She stood back up, noticing blood-soaked footprints leading further down the hall. A man's. "Tyler must have gone this way."

Hatch led the way down the hall, following the footsteps, careful to avoid stepping in the blood. They sprinted to round the corner of the long hallway, spotting the other helipad access point, and a door back into the facility a little further down.

Hatch and Cruise made their way over to a door to the facility. They'd moved through the dark passageway, barely lit by the moon in the distance and the emergency lights along the floor, following the blood-stained footsteps the entire way. Both stepped in a low squat with their guns at the ready, careful to not step on the red footprints.

In a similar fashion as to when they'd first entered the facility, Hatch took a position against the door hinges while Cruise stood by the handle. Hatch reached across from her and pulled the handle down, Cruise heading in first and clearing the hall. He stepped in line with the footprints as Hatch followed. The prints had started to fade at this point, but were clear enough to get them where they needed to go.

The footprints led them back to the engineering room, where the dragged blood from earlier had stopped. Both Cruise and Hatch leaned their ears against the door before entering. Muffled voices. Hatch tried to discern what they were saying, but it was impossible over the drone of the back-up generators.

Having switched places, Cruise stood by the hinges and cross-opened the door as Hatch led the entry, gun pointing forward and Cruise tight on her heels.

No sign of anybody. Where were Tyler and Max off to? They hadn't gotten on the crushed helicopter and left. The pilot was dead. The boat was still tied to the dock.

Wasn't it?

The whole room seemed to tilt from the bomb that had detonated earlier. Tables were strewn everywhere. Chairs were against the walls since they couldn't stay in the middle of the room without rolling away.

Moving forward another step, they heard something move. And then a voice.

"Ow!" whispered a young man. "You stepped on my foot."

"Sorry." A young woman replied.

"Freeze!" Hatch yelled. "Drop your weapons and put your hands up."

Hatch and Cruise moved closer to the voices. Their eyes were adjusting to the darkness now, and they could make out the two young adults in front of them.

Tyler Pierce and Maxine Russell. Neither had a weapon to drop, and only Tyler put his hands in the air. The pair looked terrified, like they didn't want to be here. Hatch could see by the way Tyler was fidgeting that he wanted to run, but he wouldn't get very far. Then she noticed his blood-soaked clothes. Those must have been his footsteps.

Hatch lowered her weapon and gestured for Cruise to do the same. "Where are they?" she asked them.

Max stood frozen, but Tyler looked to his right. Against the wall were Yohei and Akira Suzuki, sitting on the floor and embracing tightly next to another man Hatch didn't recognize. Then she saw the blood trail had stopped in the unfamiliar man's location. He was injured, and they'd dragged him here.

The Suzuki's looked up at Hatch and Cruise. Then, Akira stood and approached Hatch. She put a tiny palm on Hatch's scarred arm. Shivers and tingles shot up to her shoulder from the young girl, pressing on the nerve damage, even as lightly as she was.

"They're getting away," Akira said.

"Who is?" Cruise asked.

"Theo Clay and Parker Chase." Suzuki's voice sounded from the dark.

"Your partner?" Hatch asked. "He was trying to exchange money for you. Quinn Russell held your daughter for a ransom exchange."

"It was all a hoax," Suzuki said. "He took everything from me and tried to kill me. He hired those two and Quinn Russell, anonymously, to pull off this whole thing." He pointed at Tyler and Max. "Of course, those aren't the ones you should worry about at this point. We all just want to get out of here alive."

A boat engine roared to life at the dock, preparing to leave the others behind.

Before Hatch could address the wounded man on the floor or why Tyler had blood all over him, Suzuki's voice sounded from the darkness. "Go catch them. The next bomb goes off in thirteen minutes."

Hatch and Cruise bolted toward the dock.

# TWENTY-SEVEN

Hatch and Cruise raced back to the boat access door to stop Theo Clay and Parker Chase. They could still hear the boat engine below them, indicating the criminal millionaire and his security hadn't yet left the dock.

While Hatch and Cruise had been trained in speed and agility, their newfound counterparts were not as agile. Max was the closest behind and had Suzuki's arm draped over her shoulder. The billionaire had a bad knee, and while he held a cane to support him, it would not do much good in climbing down the steps quickly.

Akira followed behind them. She was younger and had no injuries or physical ailments, but her small frame could take her only so far in such a short amount of time.

Tyler and the bleeding guard were the last to descend, and the slowest moving out of all of them. Tyler wasn't small for his height and age, but having to support the entire weight of the hefty, bleeding guard slowed them down. Hatch looked back and worried they wouldn't make it in time.

Cruise ran down the stairs in front of Hatch. The boat engine, coupled with the loud backup generators around the facility made it hard to hear any conversation. The waves were getting rowdier now and splashing onto the dock. More rain poured down now than when Hatch and Cruise had watched the exchange on the helipad.

Cruise slipped on a wet step, about ten steps above the bottom, and face planted onto the ground below. Hatch jumped off the middle of the staircase to meet her partner and check he was ok. The scrappy boat engine's rumble was louder now, as was the sound of waves lapping around them. The storm was picking up. Fresh raindrops coated Hatch's face.

A bullet came whizzing toward them from the side of the boat. Hatch grabbed onto Cruise and lurched to the side of the platform to avoid the line of fire. He hopped back to his feet in a matter of seconds and ran onto the dock, Hatch on his heels. The boat roared to life in the opposite direction, back toward the Oregon coast. The two had just reached the edge of the dock as another bullet came for them. Both of them ducked to avoid it.

Hatch and Cruise still held their guns ready and aimed at the boat, getting a couple of shots off. But the boat was too far away. One shot looked like a hit, but not enough to deter the men or damage the vessel. The other shots had been blown away in the wind. No more came from Parker Chase inside the boat.

The crooked men were no longer their main concern. Hatch and Cruise worked for an agency that could find these men anywhere. There's no place they could run and hide that Talon couldn't get to. Problem was Banyan and Tracy would have no idea of the truth of the matter if they couldn't get off this ticking time bomb.

Hatch checked her watch to see how much time they had. She and Cruise had been keeping an eye on the time since they'd found out it was important.

Ten minutes.

When they'd gotten here earlier, Hatch had spotted an emergency maintenance boat on the other side of the platform. A few obstacles stood in their way—wreckage from the explosion earlier that night had crowded the direct path. They just had to get the rest of the group over all the damage and debris, and could be on their way.

The others stumbled down the steps as Hatch and Cruise helped them get on to the platform and over the damage to the emergency boat. Hatch helped Max carry Suzuki, and Cruise helped Tyler with the guard. Akira ran in between the four so as not to get lost behind them. The rain fell quicker and harder over the team. Suzuki wrapped himself around his daughter in an effort to fend off the cold. Hatch and Cruise had their wetsuits. But the rest of the group were now shivering uncontrollably.

They heard a roar of thunder followed by an unnatural crackling above them.

"Get down!" Hatch yelled. She dropped to her knees and curled into a ball, folding her head into her chest and placing her hands on her head. Everyone else followed. Cruise and Tyler folded themselves over the half-conscious guard to protect him. Max and Suzuki did the same for Akira.

The helipad above split in half. The helicopter that had sat there moments before now tumbled down with the concrete at what felt like lightspeed. It cannonballed onto the maintenance boat and sank into the ocean, sending a strong impact through the waves. The transfer station rocked wildly and threw everyone into the water in all directions.

Hatch's world went dark.

A few feet deep, she swam through the darkness and forced her eyes open. She extended her hands above her, reaching out for the platform. Finding her target, she pulled herself up to sit on the edge, which was still rocking violently. As she pulled herself out of the water, she noticed the rest doing the same. Luckily, the bleeding guard had stayed on the platform, lying flat, though sliding side to side as the vessel rocked.

Cruise yelled at her from the waves, but she couldn't hear him. She moved closer to his position.

"Fire a flare!" he yelled. "Fire a flare!"

With no hesitation, Hatch reached for a flare in her waterproof pack and fired.

There was a thump followed by an orange arc that went high into the sky. As she watched the glow disappear into the darkness, Hatch hoped Banyan would see it and that he could make it to them in under nine minutes.

## TWENTY-EIGHT

Cruise swam to the edge of the platform and pulled himself up after making sure everyone else was on. The station still rocked wildly, so everyone sat at the edge and held on for dear life. The rain whipped in every direction and changed speeds enough times that they couldn't tell whether it was drizzling or pouring. It soaked them either way, along with the wild waves splashing at them every so often.

"How much time do we have?" Hatch asked.

"Seven minutes, fifty seconds." Cruise got to his feet and spread his legs, engaging his core so the rocking platform wouldn't send him plummeting down again. "I've got no comms with Banyan. Must've been damaged when I went down with the first explosion. Better hope he saw that flare. I hope the visibility held."

"Let's get back to the engineering room. We can call for help from there," Suzuki said.

"There's no time," Cruise replied. "Anyone we call will come from inland and still be miles out by the time this thing blows."

"Why can't we just swim?" Max asked.

"That won't work. We've got a wounded guy. And there's no way to guarantee we can all swim far enough away in time. Plus, any point of land will be too far to get to by swimming." Cruise walked to the other side of the platform, hunting for the bomb. Hatch followed close behind. They found the faint orange glow nearby, on the closest pathway to the dock. The bomb was tucked into the nearest support beam.

Cruise crouched and studied the bomb intently.

"What do you think?" Hatch asked. "Can you disarm it?"

"I'd need more than seven and a half minutes. Even then, there's no way to do it without risking detonation."

"Well, what did you do in the teams? A part of being a SEAL is demolition, so what did you do when you didn't have the time?"

"We'd blow it in place," Cruise replied. "If we couldn't get far enough away for some reason, we tried to get *it* as far away from us as possible."

"How far?"

Cruise whipped his head around to take in the platform. "It won't take much to knock this thing down. The further the better. I'd say we need at least 500 meters of space."

"Think we can swim that?"

"No. Again, only a few of us are strong swimmers in the first place. We'd lose the guard and Suzuki. None of us would get far enough away in time."

"You used to swim that in seven and a half minutes."

"Yeah, not in six."

Hatch surveyed her surroundings, trying to come up with a solution. Then she heard the sound of clattering metal from the side of the platform. Getting on her stomach, she leaned over the platform to see the Swim Buddy running itself in to the side. She reached her arms down into the ocean to grab the device. "No major damage, just took a little hit when the helicopter fell, I think. We didn't have it tethered out too far."

"This'll work," Cruise replied, taking the Swim Buddy from Hatch and studying it. "Were you able to reach Banyan on your radio?"

Hatch fiddled with the handheld radio in her hand. The device was cracked along the battery casing, rendering it useless. "Mine is out of commission, too."

"Go ahead and fire another flare." Cruise stood to his feet and wiped his hands together, setting the Swim Buddy on the ground. "Everything will be fine." His cocky swagger diminished, though he made a weak attempt at a smile. More for the young girl than anyone else. "All the world's problems can be solved with a little bit of duct tape."

Hatch stopped rifling through her pack and looked at Cruise with a lifted eyebrow. "I don't think this is the right time to be making jokes."

"Any time is the right time for jokes," Cruise responded. "I'm serious, though. I think I have an idea."

"I'll leave you to it." Hatch handed Cruise a roll of duct tape and moved back to the dock to grab the flare from her pack.

Once Hatch shot the flare through the sky, she took stock of the rest of the group. All had been able to climb out of the water of their own accord, and they were still clustered together, shivered and huddled for warmth. The temperature outside the water had to be fifty-five degrees, with the water closer to forty. Not to mention the storm that was picking up all around them. Precipitation dumped from the sky as if from a giant watering can, and the wind blew in varied gusts in all directions. The waves crashed around them and onto the platform, but everyone held on to each other, keeping one another in place.

Cruise was still studying the bomb by the time Hatch's eyes landed back on him. His arms were crossed, and his brows were furrowed. One hand reached up and held his chin. Then he leaned over to grab the Swim Buddy. He sat on the platform and began duct taping the bomb onto the device.

The clock read five minutes now.

"How's it coming?" Hatch asked him, bypassing the shivering civilians to squat next to Cruise.

"I'm not sure what the best move is," Cruise replied. "The platform support out here's gotta be unstable from the first explosion. The second could easily start an underwater landslide."

"Earlier you said it'd have to be five hundred meters from us?"

"Yeah, farther, if we can help it."

"I hope it doesn't hurt the trench," Akira chimed in. Hatch and Cruise looked over in unison at Akira. They exchanged a quizzical look of puzzlement at the young girl's knowledge.

"My teacher was telling me all about the area when I told her I would be visiting. She likes to incorporate any related science or history into my lessons. Ms. Hatterly told me this water is part of the Cascadia Subduction Zone." Akira seemed to grow in confidence the more she spoke. "She said that it's capable of an earthquake that could create a tsunami wave one hundred feet high."

Hatch now had a better understanding of Fairhaven's warning drills. It also served to remind her she had unfinished business when this was all done. She owed Shyla and Maddie a better explanation of the day that changed the trajectory of all their lives, including Hatch's. "We can set the Swim Buddy's radius to 500 meters." Cruise looked back down at the bomb and the Swim Buddy it was attached to. "That should get it away from us fast enough." He looked back up at Hatch, grinning from ear to ear. Smiling back at him, she placed a hand on his shoulder as a gesture of pride. Everyone else exchanged excited murmurs at the prospect of not being blown up.

Four minutes and forty-seven seconds.

Cruise placed the Swim Buddy in the water and sent it away. He sank to the floor and sighed with relief. Hatch sat next to him as everyone cheered and continued to huddle together, waiting for their rescue from Banyan.

# TWENTY-NINE

Ed Banyan had continued sitting in the inflatable dingy since Hatch and Cruise had made their initial descent. The last bit of light was swallowed up by the ominous storm clouds, casting the sky in a net of murky darkness. Heavy rain squalls had all but obscured his view of the platform. The ocean was nothing more than a deep, dark abyss, surrounding Banyan for miles on all sides. The curtain of rain drawn around him had grown heavier with the passage of time. He checked his comms again. Nothing from Hatch or Cruise. Idling in the ocean, he fought hard against the urge to join them.

But this scenario was exactly what he was trained for.

Banyan had brought some night vision goggles for this very purpose, but they didn't do much in the way of penetrating the wall of rain separating him from his teammates. The choppy waves jostled him as he strained to get a visual beyond the horizon.

Nothing. Banyan took this as a sign to stay put until Hatch and Cruise made their way back. Or until he saw something wrong.

It had been about two hours at this point. He'd kept an eye on his phone for the time and to see if Jordan Tracy had called, but reception was spotty out on the ocean. There was nothing else to do except twiddle his thumbs and hope for the best. And remain on high alert, of course.

Just when he thought he was going to have to camp out on the water for the night, a rickety looking boat came rushing in from the direction of the transfer facility, parting the rain as it edged closer to Banyan. He hadn't been able to see it until it was just a few yards in front of him. The boat looked like it could fall apart at any second. The combination of choppy waves, wind, and rain was sure to shred it to the bone.

As it edged closer to Banyan, he realized its captain and co-captain consisted of none other than Theo Clay and Parker Chase. Apparently, they'd spotted him too, since they slowed down and stopped. Clay raised his hand as an acknowledgement.

Banyan stood to return their wave. Expecting to see the others in the back of the boat behind Clay and Chase, he saw no one. He removed his night vision goggles, in case they were causing him to miss something. The two men were close enough for him to see clearly through the rain anyway.

"What's going on?" Banyan asked them. "Where is everyone else?"

Clay bowed his head. "Our deal for the Suzuki's fell through. That terrorist group tried to kidnap us. We barely escaped with our lives."

Banyan shook his head. "But Hatch and Cruise should have been there. They'd have protected you."

Clay exchanged a glance with Chase. "I'm afraid they didn't survive the attack." He turned to look in Banyan's eyes. "They're dead."

Banyan's mind and body froze. That couldn't be right. "Dead? Are you sure?"

"As sure as a heart attack."

No, there was no way Hatch and Cruise could be dead. And why would Clay and Chase have left the Suzuki's for dead? Wouldn't the man have enough connections to call someone or arrange a boat to retrieve him if a certain amount of time had passed? Didn't he care about his partner and the future of their company?

Banyan put on his night vision goggles again and looked toward the facility. Nothing had changed from when he'd been staring at it for hours. Then again, the rain obscured visibility for miles. But he could at least make out the structure.

"I'm sorry," Clay said. Sighing, he lifted his head. "I know this is bad timing, but do you mind if we board?" Clay gestured at their dilapidated boat. "Ours is a piece of crap."

Banyan allowed the other man to distract him from his thoughts. He took his goggles back off. "Of course, come on board." He thought for a moment. "You know, in SEAL training, they teach us it's never the boat. Usually the driver." He gave a half smile. The quip received a chuckle from Clay and a look of embarrassment from Chase.

"I was never a water guy," Chase explained. "Boats aren't really my forte."

Banyan moved to start the boat's engine just as a bright orange flare shot from the direction of the facility. It rose high in the air and left a line of smoke from the waterline to the top of its orange peak before disappearing. Banyan looked over at the two men.

*Liars.*

He realized then how disheveled and wild they looked.

Clay's once-groomed hair was mussed and sticking out in all directions like a mad scientist's. His coat was unbuttoned, wrinkled, and ripped. His glasses were crooked, and blood lined the side of his mouth. Chase looked slightly more put together. Even in the darkness, the man still wore his sunglasses. But he no longer had his jacket, and his pants were wet with salt water.

Banyan looked back at Clay and Chase, wide-eyed, realizing these men were playing him and knowing he didn't understand what was actually going on. They were now his adversaries. He was met with the barrel of a gun pointed at his chest. He dove out of the way as the shot landed near its mark.

In a matter of seconds, Banyan was swallowed by the ocean. Red blood mingled with the salty water as it rose out of his body. His head felt as though it he was floating; he felt his mind slipping in and out. He fought to maintain his consciousness and looked up at the boat's location. The other men had found the engine and started it up. It began to move quickly in the direction of the coast.

Taking stock of his injury, Banyan realized the bullet hadn't hit its target, but landed just to the side. In the front of his shoulder. Salt water helped to clear injuries and mitigate risk of infection. Though it stung, the wound would be an easy enough fix.

Pushing the pain aside, he caught his breath as he floated in the choppy water. Clay and Chase were meters away already, leaving their shitty boat adrift.

Banyan swam over, boarded it, and started the engine. Revving it as fast as it could go, he headed for the transfer facility.

# THIRTY

Hatch looked out toward the shore, eyes peeled for Banyan. But there was no sign of any boat or human in view. Worry set in. Should it have been taking this long for Banyan to get to them after she'd fired the flare? With his boat, he could have gotten to them in half the time it had taken Hatch and Cruise to swim it.

She thought back to Banyan's speech.

*For the moment, we thought we were going to get a break, and then one of the instructors smiled. I'll never forget the look on his face. Through my facemask, standing there in the cold with rain pelting down on us, he smiled at us and he said, 'The only easy day was yesterday.'*

Atop the roaring waves and thunder, Hatch froze as she heard the sound of clanging metal beneath them. Hatch felt Cruise bolt upright from his slumped seat. The two exchanged looks and crawled over the platform to see into the water.

The Swim Buddy clamored with the platform, the bomb still attached.

"Shit." Cruise reached down and pulled the duct taped contraption out of the water.

The group's jubilant mood crumbled as if falling back down the giant mountain they'd just climbed.

Max and Tyler ran over to the other pair. "What is it?" Tyler asked.

Cruise studied the bomb and Swim Buddy in his hands. His expression turned to one Hatch was unable to read. Hardened. Stoic. At a loss.

Four minutes.

"The tether is on and won't let go. For some reason, it can't set the radius." Cruise chuckled and shook his head as he continued looking down. "Just like Banyan and that big surf. When it decimated everybody else, he was right there beside me."

"Well, at least he didn't try to blow you up," Hatch said.

Cruise looked at Hatch, a sad smile drawn on his face. "We have to override it."

Hatch's grin faded, meeting Cruise's expression with one of determination. "I'll do it."

Suzuki cut in, standing with his cane and Akira by his side. "Let me. You have your whole lives ahead of you, and I'll be dead soon anyway." Akira looked up at her father, shocked at his words. She gripped onto his shirt tighter.

"You have your daughter. Besides, your leg won't let you get very far." Cruise shook his head. "The point is to get as much distance from the platform as possible."

Three minutes and forty seconds.

"Shit Cruise, I'm a strong swimmer. Let me do it." Hatch raised her voice and stepped closer to Cruise, placing her hands on the Swim Buddy.

"You are a strong swimmer," Cruise said, pulling away. "But I'm stronger."

"Even if you do get far enough, your lungs will give out before you even have a chance to get back." Hatch looked into his eyes and pleaded with her own. She didn't let go of the Swim Buddy.

Cruise tugged the contraption away from her and set it down on the ground. Cupping her face with his hands, he gave her a long, tender kiss. It shot through her spine and down her arms. Her scar tingled. But something was still missing. Hatch's heart ached at how much she wished that wasn't the case.

He pulled away, still keeping her face in his hands. "I love you so much," he said. "But I know your heart has been somewhere else." Hatch looked away from him, not able to bear the pain in his eyes or conceal her guilt. But he pressed a gentle palm to turn her cheek, so she'd look at him again. "I'm not saying this to make you feel guilty. I'm saying it because maybe this is a sign that it's time for you to go where your heart belongs."

Hatch grasped Cruise's right hand in her own and squeezed it.

"And who knows," he said, stepping away but still holding her hand. "When all this is said and done, maybe I'll come out alive. And we can open that diner together."

Hatch couldn't hide the sadness that took over her features. "You have to come back. Promise me, you'll come back."

Cruise responded with a cocked smile and a wink. Then he leaned down and grabbed the Swim Buddy.

Three minutes.

The rest of the group watched on in silence as Cruise walked to the edge of the dock. Hatch followed Cruise almost to the edge but gave him enough space to jump out. The dock rocked and creaked with the weight of each of their footsteps.

He looked back at her one more time. "This does make sense for me, you know?" He quirked another smile. "I'm waterborne. At least, until I return." He gave a nod of his head at Hatch.

Nodding back at him, she stepped forward, almost willing herself to follow him into the water. Rain continued to crash down, splashing on the wooden pier at their feet.

Cruise took a deep breath and kept his eyes forward as he jumped in, the dock giving a final screech to send Cruise off. The water was too dark to see his outline swimming away, but Hatch could imagine it from when they'd spent time at the training pool. She made out the faint orange glow of the bomb's timer, moving in the opposite direction and gliding deeper into the ocean. He moved fast with the help of the Swim Buddy.

"What do we do now?" Suzuki asked.

"We wait."

Hatch's heart sank to her stomach, and she allowed her knees to buckle as it crashed down on her like a tidal wave. Cruise entered the water, knowing full well he wouldn't have time to make it back out.

The orange glow moved further and further away from her as Hatch let herself collapse from her standing position. Her knees couldn't handle the tremendous weight on her shoulders. She felt as though she'd been carrying it for decades. And maybe she had been.

She'd lost her twin sister recently, though they had been estranged for a while. Prior to that, the last loved one she'd experienced dying was her father, over twenty years ago. Though the initial aching pain from their deaths had subsided, there wasn't a day that had gone by where she didn't miss them, long to hear their voice, or go on runs with her father. Would she feel the same about Cruise?

She wished she'd just told him she loved him and opened up to him unconditionally. About her thoughts and fears, about her hesitations and doubts, even about Savage.

Savage.

What did this mean for her and Savage now? Had it been Savage all along?

It wasn't fair to think like that right now. Cruise was sacrificing his life for everyone there. For her. He didn't hesitate once, knowing well what would happen.

Her chest was so numb, she could barely feel her heart throbbing against it. The scene in front of her was dark. The rain had subsided somewhat, but the waves still lapped wildly. The wind had also died down, but she could still feel the cool breeze brush against her cheek. It was still warm from when Cruise had held it. She reached up to graze it with her fingers.

Her mind was filled with the waves again. All these what ifs. What if she'd just stayed with Savage in the first place? What if she'd said yes to Cruise, to open a diner? Would they have run off without even finishing the op? What if they'd found the bomb in time, or the Swim Buddy before everything crashed down on it, on them?

She allowed herself to fill with guilt, anger, sadness, remorse, regret. All these emotions she didn't know what to do with. She didn't know how to handle them. They seemed to fill her body, and it built up in her legs, her stomach, her arms, and her chest. They swelled in her mind, and she wanted to scream, or cry, or break something just to let them loose.

Emotions were something she wasn't accustomed to. Always letting them hover just beneath the surface, then pushing them back down again.

They didn't get her far in her line of work. It never ceased to amaze her how confident she was in her ability to move through a life-or-death situation with the speed and agility she'd learned in the military. But when it came to dealing with emotions, all she knew was avoidance.

But here she was, watching her ex from years past and partner from the last few months disappear into the inky black abyss. Emotions bubbled inside her and continued to claw their way out.

Maybe years of repression meant they'd all come back eventually anyway. And hit much harder. Coupled with the feeling of loss and regret, she was experiencing things she'd never thought to consider or imagine.

In a daze, she checked the watch on her wrist, having synced it to the bomb's timer before Cruise departed. He'd been out there for over two minutes. She felt each ticking of the second hand as time dwindled below the one-minute mark.

Hatch held her breath and hoped beyond reason Cruise would find his way back to her.

# THIRTY-ONE

Hatch stared at the raging sea, scanning the dark surface for any sign of Cruise as the seconds ticked by. "That man is one of the bravest I've seen in a long time." Yohei Suzuki broke Hatch out of her thoughts and placed a gentle hand on her left shoulder.

"You're telling me." Hatch allowed a faint smile to play on her lips, welcoming Suzuki's distraction from her inner ocean.

"He meant something more to you. I see that now."

She looked at Suzuki. His expression was warm and sympathetic. She welcomed it. "We had dated a few years back and just lost touch. Then he came back into my life more recently, but"—she looked back out at the water—"I don't know. It just didn't click. The timing maybe. But I didn't put in the effort he deserved."

"Do you wish you had?" Suzuki asked. "Do you wish things had… clicked?"

"More than anything." Hatch breathed heavily, allowing the light rain to coat her face.

"Maybe he'll make it back." Akira slid her hand into Hatch's and sat beside the woman, looking at her with the hope and innocence only a child could hold in her expression.

Hatch's right arm tingled as the girl tightened her grip and leaned her head against Hatch's right shoulder. The sensation shot through her wrist, up her forearm, all the way to her shoulder. Not the sharp zing it used to be, but noticeable nerve damage. A reminder of when she'd hesitated all those years ago. Then when she'd hesitated in Alaska. And again, just earlier today, the decision that led them to all this.

To Cruise's sacrifice.

Hatch was caught off guard by the aching feeling in her chest. All the emotions had ignored her request to stay hidden with the rest of her pain.

She looked up as a boom sounded across the water. Hatch checked her watch. The bomb had gone off right on time. Zero minutes left.

A half sphere of ocean shot up into the sky across from the dock, way in the distance. Five hundred meters. It was not close enough to damage the structure, but just enough to rock it harder.

Hatch hoped Cruise was on his way back, that he didn't get caught in the explosion. That he raced away from it in time.

Akira buried her face into Hatch's right shoulder. Her small presence reminded Hatch of her niece, Daphne. The way Daphne had held her hand and clung so tight when she'd last hugged her. The memory hit her like a ton of bricks as Akira leaned into Hatch.

Suzuki's grip tightened on Hatch's left shoulder. The child began to shake with soft sobs that shook Hatch to her core. She didn't process anything for the next few moments. Her mind went blank, and her body numb. She could no longer feel the girl sobbing into her or the older man comforting her with his hand on her shoulder. Hatch had the sensation as though she'd left her body, and she wasn't sure if she'd make it back.

Eventually the sobbing quieted, and the girl lifted herself off Hatch.

Hatch's vision was blurred from the rain, and maybe the tears trying to escape her eyes, but she could just make out the shape of a boat and its low hum, approaching the dock.

The boat Theo Clay and Parker Chase had escaped in appeared in front of her. She still sat on the dock, cradled by little Akira and Suzuki. She retreated from her own mind as the boat inched closer. Expecting the two criminals, Hatch edged away from the Suzuki's and pulled out her gun. To her surprise, Ed Banyan popped his head out the side of the boat.

He leaped onto the dock. "I thought you guys could use a lift," he said with a wide grin on his face. The smile dropped as he surveyed the group. Hatch couldn't see behind her, but she didn't imagine anyone feeling particularly happy, given the circumstances.

After Banyan had observed everyone else through the pouring rain, his eyes fell back onto Hatch. "Where's Cruise?" She could barely hear his question over the new bout of rain pelted the dock.

Hatch tried to come up with the words, but nothing escaped her mouth when she opened it. A single tear fell from her eye and mixed with the rain spraying on her face.

Banyan took a step back, as if he'd been punched in the stomach. He turned to face away from the group, holding his face in his hands.

Hatch moved from her seat and remembered her combat breathing techniques. Two deep inhales, one smooth, long exhale. This technique had been taught to override the fight-or-flight response, to bring oxygen from the amygdala in the back of the brain to the prefrontal cortex. This way, Hatch could make decisions from an objective viewpoint. It would be unwise to trust a shaken nervous system with any kind of life-or-death decision-making.

Akira let go as Hatch approached Banyan. She laid a hand on his shoulder and the man turned his head to face hers. The pained expression on his face spoke volumes as to how he felt about Cruise's fate. But Hatch knew they held the fate of five others in their hands. Life, and its preservation, took precedence over her suffering. At least for the moment. Like every battlefield she'd ever walked, moving forward in the face of tragedy was a warrior's burden. She inhaled deeply, feeling Cruise in the salty air filling her lungs as she did her best to soldier on.

"Thanks for coming back for us," Hatch said.

Banyan took a deep breath of his own and allowed his features to soften into a smaller smile than the one he'd held just a few minutes ago. "Sure thing."

Hatch smiled back, then her eyes trailed to the wound on his shoulder. "What happened there?"

"Oh that?" He looked down toward the bullet hole with feigned surprise. "That's from our old pals, Theo Clay and Parker Chase. Had a nice run-in with them earlier. Really stand-up guys. Tried to kill me, and then stole my boat."

"I guess that explains why you came in on something different. And why it took so long."

"Yeah. They stole my boat. I stole theirs. Tried to tell me everyone was dead, and that The Watch tried to kill them."

Hatch let out a soft chuckle. "Not entirely a lie. But their motives were dirtier than we realized. Let's get that gunshot wound taken care of. Don't want you to lose any more blood." She headed over to Max for the med kit and applied gauze to the man's shoulder.

"Let's get everyone loaded," he said.

"You think this boat will hold all of us?"

"We don't have a choice. I've definitely ridden in better, but also ridden in worse. I think this'll work best if everyone spreads out to distribute the weight evenly."

Hatch looked over the shivering crowd, trying to determine who needed to go on first. Suzuki was injured but could hold his own for the most part. That guard, however, was still losing a lot of blood, even with the amount of gauze he had on.

"Let's get him to the middle." Hatch went over to the guard lying on the ground and grabbed his arms. Banyan grabbed his legs, and they carried him across the dock onto the boat. "You guys can follow us on and start clearing out some excess. We want to make sure this boat doesn't have to carry more than just our weight."

The group followed Hatch and Banyan on and began clearing out extra cargo. Wooden boxes, large fishing nets, and several rods were cast aside. When they were finished, Hatch walked out onto the dock one last time.

Banyan poked his head outside the boat to look at Hatch. "You ready?"

She continued looking out at the water. Her fingers grazed her scar. "Not yet."

Banyan sighed as sorrow filled his eyes. "It's been four minutes."

Four whole minutes since the bomb had gone off. Since Cruise had sacrificed himself. Since Hatch's life had changed in a way she'd never even considered.

Hatch struggled to peel herself away from the edge of the dock.

She boarded the boat and received a pat on the back from Banyan. "I'll have you stand at the bow," he said. "You can be our eyes in the front and guide us in."

Hatch looked around at everyone else. They each stood equidistant from each other and the center of the boat. The wounded guard laid in the center. She took up her own position at the bow.

Banyan started the engine and glided the boat back toward the coast. A wave of relief seemed to hit the group all at once, since everyone relaxed against whatever wall of the boat they were closest to. Hatch was feeling ready to get back as well, but she wished Cruise would have been able to join her.

They'd reached the area where Banyan had deployed Hatch and Cruise earlier. In less than an hour's time, Hatch's world had been rocked to its core. The rain cleared enough for Hatch to see the faint glow of the facility's flashing red light atop the radio tower. The chop of the water lapped at the rickety boat's side, but otherwise, silence filled the air. It was short-lived. A low rumble sounded in the distance back toward the platform. The water became angry with motion, rocking the boat violently.

"Was there another bomb?" Tyler asked.

They were all silent for a moment as they processed the noise they'd just heard.

The group on the boat began to panic and screams and panting filled the stunned silence.

A black wall of water rose above the twenty-foot-tall transfer facility, looming high and then swallowing it whole.

# THIRTY-TWO

Parker Chase sat at the back of the stolen boat and steered through the rocky outcrops. Right in front of him was Theo Clay. He could just barely make out the other man in the dark, the rain pummeling him.

"I should have hired someone who could do these things right," Clay said.

"Maybe you should have." Chase leveled a steely gaze at the older man.

Clay looked his security detail in the eye, then began laughing hysterically. Chase let him process their current state however he needed to. He was just trying to get them to shore before the nuclear facility went down. Chase was trying to save his own ass just as much as—if not more than—Theo Clay's.

"What a disaster." Clay shook his head and stared out at the ocean, in the direction of the facility behind them. "I knew it was a risk getting that group to abduct Suzuki and the kid, but I never imagined it turning out like this. I thought the team from Talon would just drop the matter and let me handle it. Fools." He smoothed out his jacket and rebuttoned his cufflinks, as though the ocean and rain hadn't already damaged the expensive attire. "I thought the location would be secure enough to get in and kill everyone before getting back. It doesn't matter now, no one should be able to tie this back to us." He rubbed his palms together and blew into them, trying to conduct a natural heat, then chuckled again. "Who knew that guy Quinn was going to be such a loose cannon? It could've gone a lot worse."

"How's that?" Chase asked, having to raise his voice for Clay to hear him over the crashing waves and rain. The tone ebbed in his body and made him feel the anger swelling up. "All things considered, it couldn't have gone worse. Gonna be a hell of a job trying to spin this thing."

"Oh, don't worry about it," Clay said. "We'll just blame it all on those environmentalists. Yes. They abducted the Suzuki's and tried to kill them at the site, then throw them in the ocean so no one would ever know. It'll be perfect. And when that bomb drops that platform, it will be just a tragedy of a hostage negotiation gone bad, and we're the sole survivors. We'll be touted as heroes, and we're a hundred million dollars richer. Unless…" Clay put a finger to his mouth, deep in thought. "What if the bomb doesn't detonate? What if they all come back alive? Maybe they've radioed for help."

Chase sighed. "The bomb will detonate. I doubt they'd be able to disarm it without also detonating it. And if for some reason, it doesn't go off, I'll spin this boat around and finish the job myself."

"Even so, what if they're able to radio for help or get a message to someone before the bomb goes off?"

"That's not possible."

Clay squinted his eyes, straining in the dark as he peered back in the direction of the transfer station. "How can you be so sure?"

"Because I took care of it. They can't radio for help because I placed a signal jammer when we first landed the helicopter." He took his hand off the throttle, dropping the speed of the boat and grabbing Clay's attention.

"I'm glad you're on my team."

"Team?" Chase let the anger in his normally stoic voice rise above the wind and chop of the rough water slapping the sides of the boat. "Since when did this become a 'we' scenario? You paid me to do a job which I did…did well. But you never said anything about a hundred million dollars."

"This became a 'we scenario' when you agreed to work for me. Yes, I created the plans, but you went along with them. You've earned plenty. You can stop your whining."

The wind and rain splashed in their faces as the boat slowed to a halt in the middle of the ocean, still miles from the shoreline. Chase straightened his form and stared at his employer with disbelief. The boat rocked more now than it had while they were moving. The rain poured straight down on them instead of sideways.

Clay looked over at him and narrowed his eyes. "What do you think you're doing?"

"I think it's time to renegotiate the terms of our agreement."

Clay laughed at the other man. "Please. This really isn't enough for you?" He kicked the briefcase containing one million dollars. It banged against an oar on the floorboard and came to rest between the two men.

"No." Chase took his hand off the tiller and folded his arms against his chest. The boat rocked, but Chase remained balanced, poised to strike. "Not when I know it's one percent of everything you took from Suzuki."

Clay sat frozen. Fear replaced his defiant look. He choked out a laugh and rolled his eyes. "Fine. You want five million? I'll give you that. Nothing but a mere fraction, that's fine."

"I want ten."

"Ten? Million?" Clay stared at the other man with wild eyes.

"You'll still be walking away with ninety," Chase said. "It's going to take a hell of a lot of money to get me to disappear without so much as a groan when all this is over."

"Just start this boat already." Clay shivered. His eyes darted between his watch and the gun on the side of Chase's hip as he sat nervously on the bench seat. "I don't want to be out here anymore. I have people to meet tomorrow morning."

"It's agreed then." Chase restarted the engine and went back to steering. "Has the transfer been confirmed yet?"

"No," Clay said. "That's something I'll discuss in my meeting tomorrow."

"Got it." Chase was silent for a moment. "I think I'll disappear when this is all over. Go off to an island somewhere."

"Marvelous." Clay clapped his hands in mock admiration for his security detail's future plans. "I think I'll take over the world. But right now, how about we get the hell off this water and put as much distance as possible between us and that godforsaken transfer station?"

Off in the distance behind them, a loud boom sounded. A half-sphere of dark liquid shot up from the surface of the ocean, away from the nuclear transfer facility. Large waves began to roll toward them.

"Sounds like that idiot Quinn took care of our problems. Time to move." Clay gave a weak smile before turning his back to Chase.

Chase turned his attention to the transfer station. In the distance, he saw the faint, but distinct red hue of the helipad tower light. Something was wrong. The structure was supposed to crumble after the explosion. The fact it was still standing meant they had a problem. A big one.

He brought the engine back to life. But instead of pressing on toward the shore, he yanked the handle and turned the boat back in the direction they had come from.

"You're turning back?" Clay asked.

"The Hatch woman and Alden Cruise must've found the bomb and moved it. Not sure how they did it, but they managed to get the bomb far enough away before detonation."

"Impossible." Clay couldn't hide the panic in his face.

"That's why people like them are hired. To do the impossible." Chase kicked himself for not taking the time to finish the job himself.

"What are you going to do?"

"I'm going to finish this thing once and for all." Chase rested a hand on the pistol on his hip. "I'm going to show you why I'm worth the extra money you're going to pay me when this is done."

"Well, make it fast. I don't want to be anywhere near that place when the sun rises."

Chase had moved the boat across the water toward the transfer facility. After several minutes of motoring, his heart skipped a beat when he saw the towering structure vanish into darkness.

"See? You worry too much. The station's gone. Just needed to be patient." Clay squinted through the rain at the giant liquid wall hurdling toward them. "Wait. What's that? A wave?"

"That's not like any wave I've ever seen." Chase spun the boat away from the fast-approaching wall of black water. He opened up the throttle, and the boat's motor roared. There was no doubt in Parker Chase's mind they were now in a race for their lives.

## THIRTY-THREE

The giant tsunami wave pulled the boat back toward it, threatening to devour the small vessel and everyone inside it. The small waves generated by the wind had all but subsided. Bursts of lightning illuminated the sky and loud crackles of thunder sounded overhead.

Salt water sloshed heavily into the boat, soaking everyone, and Banyan yelled, "We need to start bailing."

Hatch, in the bow, heard him. Turning, the blinding waves and rain blurred her vision, but she could make out shapes. There was no way, anyone could bail.

Suzuki kept his cane in one hand and managed to balance with the other, holding on to the wall as the water splashed at his feet. Akira cried and tried to inch closer to her father, but with each step she took, the waves jostled her backwards. Max's and Tyler's faces held expressions of fear and uncertainty, but they stayed close together and braved the madness of the storm.

Banyan remained at the helm, kicking the boat into overdrive. His bullet wound didn't seem to be of any concern as he remained upright and determined to get the boat back to shore. Hatch tried to direct him on a path away from the rocky outcrops.

Hatch looked back at where the platform had been. The wave had devoured it completely. If it hadn't been raining, Hatch still wouldn't have been able to see any of the structure's remains. It belonged to the ocean now.

They were about two miles from where the structure had been. The black wall of water flew toward them at what felt like light speed, about a mile away, and rushing closer by the second.

Hatch looked ahead toward the coast. The giant wave behind them was drawing water up from the shoreline, a natural watery monster trying to become bigger and more powerful to increase destruction. Hatch began to feel the boat stall as the force of the water behind them threatened to pull them closer.

She yelled at the top of her lungs to Banyan to be heard over the crashing waves and falling rain. "We have to outrun this thing!"

Banyan looked behind him at the approaching tsunami. "We can't," he yelled back. He was already pushing the boat to its max. There was no way they could go any faster. No way they could survive this.

This had to be the end.

Banyan furrowed his brows in thought, and a moment later, his expression shifted to one of determination. "Everyone, hold on," he yelled. Then he turned the wheel hard to the left. Groans sounded from every passenger. Hatch noticed Max and Tyler fall into each other and then swiftly move back to their original positions. The guard on the bottom slid on the slippery floor, though he was heavy enough that he didn't move too much.

"What are you doing?" Suzuki yelled across the way. "We have to outrun it, that has to be the way."

"No," Banyan replied. "There's no way this boat can handle that. Our only chance at surviving is to crest this thing, and we can't do that unless we get to the lowest end, to the left."

"Can we even make that?" Hatch asked, still gripping the side. "It's coming toward us, and fast."

"When flight's not an option," Banyan said, "I choose fight."

"What's the plan?" Hatch asked.

"We're gonna run parallel to the wave, and we have to ride the curl. Hatch, I need you to stay up front and look out for the lowest point of the wave. The sweet spot where we can try to mount it. Everyone needs to shift their weight to the port side of the boat."

Banyan looked at Hatch, his hands still gripped at the wheel. "Hatch." His voiced called her attention. "Did Cruise ever tell you about our boat crew?"

"He didn't."

"Well, he would've told you that we never lost a race because it pays to be a winner."

"Great," Hatch yelled. "I don't plan on losing today."

---

THE SMALL BOAT surfed along the giant wave, growing higher second by second. Banyan kept his eyes on Hatch, who kept her eyes forward. Everyone stayed at their posts, weighing the boat down on the left to keep it from tipping over into the wave.

Dawn hadn't yet broken, and the storm brewed as if to shove the circumstances in their faces. Hatch's eyes and body had already adjusted to the present surroundings but navigating the wave would still be a feat. Her training was mostly land-based, so in this case, she was trusting her gut and hoping for the best.

"Use the bowline to strap in," Banyan called out to Hatch. "We want to find where the peak is nine feet or lower."

She tied the rope in front of her to her waist to stay put in her section. Her body was now tight against the front of the boat. Her eyes searched for the lowest point of the wave, still farther ahead than she'd like it to be. The wall of water was right beside them. Hatch was sure if she put her hand in the water, it would glide through her fingers—if not rip them right off from the force.

The boat hydroplaned as it rode sideways through the massive wave. Its passengers jostled around, fighting to not fall overboard. The guard in the center of the boat was safe, but he slid more now, and his weight shifted the boat's balance in the water. Every time he crashed against the frames, he lost more blood. It had oozed through the gauze at this point and stained anything it touched. The man had faded in and out of consciousness throughout the night, but now he was out cold. They had only so much time to get him back to the mainland for medical attention.

Banyan hit a rough patch of water, causing the guard to slide and bump harder than he had been. In a rush of heroism, Tyler leapt from his post to shelter the bleeding man and help him stay in place. The boat was lighter on the port side now, causing the vessel to lift and tilt away from the wave. Just what they'd been trying to avoid.

Hatch looked back at the young man and called, "What are you doing?"

"I thought he needed my help," Tyler replied.

Suzuki and Akira joined Max to put more weight on the side and lean it the other way, to no avail. They needed the guard in the center again, and Tyler's weight to balance it out. But the young man was trapped in the middle, trying to keep the guard from sliding and unable to stand with the rocky waves bouncing beneath them.

In a last-ditch effort, Hatch wrapped her scarred arm into the bowline as a measure to make sure she didn't fall off, lifted a leg over the side of the boat and straddled the outside, now facing the opposite direction than she had been.

The boat's weight was redistributed, and Banyan was able to sail smoother than before. The choppiness had diminished, and the vessel glided through the water with only a few notches of turbulence.

Hatch turned her head to see the front again. She noticed the frothy white of the wave's crest. "We're closing in on the low end." She turned back to Banyan. "Just another hundred meters or so."

Banyan furrowed his brows and gripped the wheel until his knuckles turned white.

Akira clung to her father on the side of the boat as he gripped the siding and huddled against Max's back. Everyone was drenched in rain and seawater. When all this was over, they'd look ten years older than when the day had begun.

White water began to descend and curl over them. Banyan turned his head to look back at everyone. "I can't hold her steady for long. Brace yourselves!"

The group huddled closer together and hoped.

Banyan turned the boat hard into the wave, hitting the crest. Water crashed onto everyone and landed in all compartments of the vessel. The motor strained and sputtered as the bow of the boat faced skyward, turning almost completely vertical. Hatch clung to the front as the rope dug into her arm and waist. Tyler and the guard slid toward the back and Tyler had to hold on to the eyelet on the floor. The rest still clung to the siding, almost hanging off.

After what seemed like a lifetime, the boat broke free from the wave's crest. They slid down the backside of the mountainous black wall and reached the low point where the sea leveled off. Banyan continued to steer the boat in the opposite direction of the surging water. The ocean's chop was a welcome sight after the ferocity they'd just experienced.

There was no sign of the transfer station. It was now sealed beneath the deep black of the water's surface, entombed by the vast ocean. The same dark grave that now held Cruise. Hatch fought against her own wave of despair, pushing back the flood of emotion seeking to crash down upon her.

With the threat of the tsunami neutralized, Banyan slowed the boat. An unsettling calm filled the air. He slowly turned the boat to face the shore. Hatch watched as the dark wall of water headed toward the inlet, and the small town of Fairhaven just beyond.

Hatch took stock of the ragtag group of survivors. They remained huddled. The fear and panic that fueled the adrenaline of their recent brush with death had receded. Instant fatigue apparent in each face. They had all been involuntarily indoctrinated into the world where Hatch spent the better part of her life. Each was now left to recover from the scars of battle, both internal and external, which they'd carry from this day forward. And each with their own burden to shoulder.

The rain had slowed down. Suzuki had his eyes closed, and he kissed the top of Akira's head. She'd been crying, her tears mixing with the rain. Hatch thought of her own father. His devotion came in the gift of each encounter she survived. She felt him with her now, as she always did. Hatch knew Cruise had now taken his post alongside him. His final sacrifice was the truest display of love. No words could ever speak so loudly or resonate so clearly. She'd wished in the deepest part of her soul, that she had been able to reciprocate.

Max stared at Tyler with wide eyes, the events of the past twenty-four hours passing back and forth between the two without words. Fear, anger, and loss carried by each, in varying degrees. Beneath it all, Hatch recognized another expression. Guilt. The weight of which pulled at Tyler's shoulders like an anchor. But through all of it, Hatch saw something else. She saw an inner strength. A steady resolve, mirroring that of the young man's brother-in-law. For all the wrong Tyler had done, he had proven himself in those final critical moments, when life and death were on the line. He made the right decision under fire. And for that, Graham would have been proud.

As Hatch shifted her gaze out toward the Fairhaven shore, she spotted Banyan's stolen boat. Too far to see clearly, she knew Theo Clay and Parker Chase were onboard. Her trigger finger itched for justice as she turned to Banyan. "They're getting away." She cursed at the angry ocean separating her from the vengeance coursing through her veins.

Banyan began steering the boat back to shore, following the force of nature leading the way. He eyed the fleeing vessel just beyond the wave's crest and then back at Hatch. "I don't think so," he said. "Karma's a real bitch sometimes. And they're about to learn a one-time lesson."

Hatch felt the pull of the ocean. In it, she felt Cruise. He was now one with its power. And he was about to unleash hell on the enemy.

## THIRTY-FOUR

THE DARK WALL OF WATER WAS NOW CLOSING IN BEHIND PARKER CHASE AND Theo Clay, catching up to them by the minute. It was so dark, it blended in with the pre-dawn sky and pouring rain. Thunder clapped above them, almost loud enough for them to hear over the roaring noise of rough waves crashing against one another.

Chase remained silent and did the best he could to move the boat in the other direction as Clay barked orders left and right. "Steer in the other direction!" "What are you doing? Haven't you ever steered a boat before? Weren't you trained in this? Can you go any faster? I'm about to vomit from all this rocking."

As a former Special Forces operator, Chase never had much training in the way of guiding a boat over a choppy ocean in a brewing storm. He'd told Clay as much after shooting the guy from Talon and making a quick getaway. Most of Chase's training and duties took place on land, in varying biomes of the world. The ocean had rarely been one of them, if ever.

Chase had revved the engine to its maximum speed, trying to will the vessel to move faster than the giant wave encroaching on them.

"Go faster!" Clay yelled again.

"This is as fast as it goes," Chase yelled back. "I've told you that already." The boat had now reached a buoy just a few miles from the shoreline. Almost there. Just a few more minutes, and they'd be able to grab the money and run into town and take shelter.

The boat slowed as it approached the shore. "What are you doing?" Clay yelled again.

Behind them, the tsunami wave gathered more water from the nearby inlet, allowing it to grow wider and higher. The boat's motor began to sputter, making popping noises they could just barely hear over all the other clamor. For every foot the boat moved forward, the monster of a wave pulled it one foot back. They were stuck in neutral, going nowhere,

Clay's eyes widened against the pelting rain. Shivers took hold of his entire body, and he shook violently. "Get this thing out of the water now, or I'll throw it all in the ocean!" He stood up in the shaky vessel, losing his balance and tripping more than once, and held the briefcase off the side, over the water. Chase gave the other man a deadpan stare, daring him to do it, though not caring either way. Chase had decided his future plans already, and he could achieve them with or without Clay's stolen cash. The extra million was just a bonus.

Clay looked Chase in the eyes just as a rough patch of water jostled the boat upward and almost tossed Clay off. He landed stomach-first over the side as the waves rocked him back and forth. His head jostled side to side, and his hands reached down in the water, whipping whichever direction the wave was pulling. Clay brought his hands back up to grip the siding, and he heaved the contents of his stomach over the side of the boat.

Chase stifled a laugh.

Clay wiped the bile off his mouth and turned his head to look at the dark liquid wall fast approaching them.

Chase looked ahead to the shore. He could see the lighthouse's stream of light move back and forth across the ocean, calling any sailors into shore. Tsunami sirens blared in the distance, but the sound was almost completely drowned out by the noisy ocean.

The motor still popped loudly against the waves and storm. "Why can't you make this damn thing go faster?" Clay growled at Chase as he gripped the side of the boat with all the strength in his hands.

"I told you," Chase said, not turning to look at Clay. "This is as fast as it can go. I'm trying to outrun it."

"Well, try harder!"

Chase looked back at the massive wall, now feet behind them. "We're gonna have to ride it."

"We're what?" Clay's face was contorted into something resembling anger and disgust, but deep in his eyes, Chase saw the fear in the older man that he tried so hard to cover with money.

Chase steered the boat to face the direction the tsunami was headed. The motor finally gave out as the giant wave swept the boat into its strong pull, as though the water were a massive tow truck dragging the vessel up a liquid road. The boat began turning vertically and riding higher as the tall wave continued to suck it into its endless vortex.

"We're at twenty feet!" Chase yelled before the crest collapsed on them, dragging them through the other side of the wave.

The last sounds Parker Chase ever heard were those of the boat crashing through the water. Through the inky darkness, he saw fragments of the vessel and everything inside it float away from him. Trying to swim to the surface was no use. He was churned by the unstoppable tower of water until he was forced to surrender.

In whipping darkness, he slammed into something hard, forcing the last reserve of oxygen from his depleted lungs. In the frothy mix of whitewater, he saw what had struck him. Theo Clay's face, pale as moonlight, whipped wildly before him. Panic ravaged his eyes. Clay grabbed hold of Chase, his arms cinching tight around him.

Chase was a life-preserver to his boss. But there was no life to preserve. Chase inhaled deeply, taking in a lung full of water. He choked; his body shook violently. He mustered the last bit of strength to break free of Clay's grasp.

Chase kicked hard, fighting against the burning fire of his oxygen-deprived muscles as he sought the surface. All hope dashed as he felt a hand grip his ankle. Clay sealed his fate, becoming an anchor and dragging him downward into the deep abyss as he became one with the darkness surrounding him.

# THIRTY-FIVE

The darkness that shrouded the team just moments ago was now giving way to an early morning glow. Overcast clouds still hung low in the sky, transforming it into a deep gray. The storm had moved on, leaving cooler air, and the precipitation was now barely a sprinkle.

Hatch watched as the tsunami swallowed Theo Clay and Parker Chase. The SEAL boat came out on the other side completely fragmented, with no sign of its passengers. She applauded the two men for not giving up without a fight but pitied them for not recognizing the best way to evade the wave was to ride with it, not against it. Although, if she were out here on her own, she wasn't so sure she wouldn't have made the same fatal mistake.

She moved to the guard in the middle of the boat and checked his pulse. It was faint, just a pinprick of a vibration against the tips of her fingers. "He needs medical attention soon," Hatch said to Banyan. After a moment to catch his breath, Banyan didn't hesitate to start the boat back up and head for shore.

Max approached the guard and began applying pressure to the wound again. Tyler still sat next to the bleeding man.

Hatch used this as a moment to give the young adults some privacy, though she could still hear their hushed conversation. She would have taken the guard with her, but he wasn't conscious enough to know what was going on, anyway.

Tyler was propped up on his hands. The young man's sodden clothes now clung to his skin. The remnants of Quinn Russell's blood had been washed away by the ocean and rain. "So," he said.

Max glanced up at him, wearing a slight smile. "So."

"That was—"

"Yeah." Max chuckled. "Maybe we should talk about it later. After we get off the boat."

Tyler chuckled in return and nodded his head.

"Well, I do have to ask you." She tucked a strand of drenched red hair behind her ear. "What happened with my brother?"

Tyler sighed and looked down at his lap. "He was going to kill me, Max." His voice was calm but firm. "I didn't shoot him first. He was going to detonate the second bomb with the same remote. I knocked it away from him. Then he pointed the rifle at me and I tried to get that away from him too and then… and then it went off while it was pointed at him."

Max didn't hide her sad expression. "I don't know what to say. I'm so sorry he tried to kill you."

"Me too," Tyler said.

Max used her free hand to take hold of Tyler's. "Everything happens for a reason, I think."

Hatch turned her attention to the coast. The same tsunami sirens she'd heard the other day had come back alive. She could hear them in the distance. The faint but deafening blare.

As the large wave moved closer to the shore, it had gained more height and speed than when it first engulfed the transfer facility structure. It crashed into the shoreline and made its way inland. Hatch felt powerless watching the natural elements. As much as she wanted to swoop in and save the whole town from the massive wave, that wasn't within her control. Even if she saved some people, it was unrealistic to believe she could save them all.

Tyler's voice sounded from behind her. "I hope they're ok."

Hatch looked back at the young man. From the remorseful expression on his face, she knew he could only be talking about a few certain individuals. His mother, his sister, and his niece.

"They'll be alright," Hatch said. "The tsunami wasn't high enough to have too severe an impact, though I can't speak to the physical damage on the buildings. But the storm's already died down enough." She attempted a reassuring smile, but after losing Cruise, everything she did came out flat. But sometimes false hope was the only hope left. All she could muster was, "We'll be there soon enough.

Tyler nodded and turned his attention back to the guard.

The truth was, Hatch was worried about the family, too. The storm had been wild, at least out on the ocean. She could only imagine that it hit the coast with the same ferocity. She would never be able to forgive herself if something had happened to Graham Benson's family. Tyler Pierce and the Bensons had already suffered so much loss. They didn't deserve to suffer anymore.

Tyler sat motionless, a quiet reserve evident on his face. Holding his head with his hands, he grumbled something inaudible. Words only meant for himself.

It was Suzuki who sought to console the young man, resting his hand gently on his shoulder. "What you did for my daughter is a debt I plan to repay. I have the best attorneys in the world at my beck and call. I'll ensure that you don't set foot in a prison."

The words seemed to only worsen the strain. Tyler lifted his head. His eyes moistened. "I killed Dibner."

The words sent a hush over the group. Suzuki kept his hand in place, but his body stiffened.

"I didn't want to. Quinn forced me." He looked at Max. She sat numbly beside him. "He made me bury him alive." The words caused his voice to crack, and a tear rolled down his face.

Before anyone could find the words, Tyler continued. "But I tried to save him. After Quinn left, I went back to my sister's van and grabbed a piece of PVC pipe and put it in the ground as an air hole. I intended to go back and dig him up. But Quinn had other plans."

Suzuki hugged his daughter a little tighter.

"I was worried the rain would drown him. I remembered a time when I went snorkeling with Graham. It was raining heavy that day. And he put on an attachment that blocked the water from entering. So, I put an elbow joint on the end to make sure he'd be okay until I got back."

Tyler's voice dropped to a mumble. Hatch looked at the young man, his face was ghostly pale, almost a light green, and he sat facing Max.

Max's lips set into a tight line. She closed her eyes. Tyler was looking down at his lap. He couldn't bring himself to look at Suzuki.

Silence fell over the group, with the only sound the distant waves crashing and the pattering of rain landing on the boat. Hatch and Banyan exchanged glances before observing everyone else. Suzuki was on the brink of tears. Akira still had her face buried in her father's chest, but now she shook. Hatch's gaze then fell on Tyler. The young man's face was ridden with guilt and sorrow. She remembered seeing a picture of him with Graham Benson at Shyla's house. They both looked so happy and carefree. A stark contrast to now with Benson deceased and Tyler involved with an extremist group.

"If there's anything I've learned in my experience, it's that anything's possible." Hatch's words of hope lifted some of the burden in Tyler's eyes. She couldn't help but feel some of the weight herself. If Graham had been alive, she was sure Tyler wouldn't have gone down the path he was on now. The fracture left in the wake of Graham's death had a ripple effect, and she was bearing witness to one of those ripples now.

"If there's a chance he's still alive, then I have to go to him." Tyler looked up at Hatch, and around at everyone else.

Suzuki seemed to snap out of his saddened trance. "What do you mean?"

Everyone looked at Tyler. Max's eyes were wide with hope. Hatch noticed the younger woman's breaths were now deeper than they had been.

Hatch cut into the moment. "Where's he buried?"

"Not far," Tyler said. Pointing in the direction of a field just off the shoreline. "In the marsh. Just beyond the bend."

Hatch looked in the direction his finger was pointing. "Banyan, let's head that way."

"On it." Banyan turned the boat's trajectory slightly sideways from where they were already heading.

"Let's just hope we're not too late." Hope was a luxury Hatch rarely afforded herself, but it was the only thing she could offer. Seeing the desperation in the young man's eyes, she knew that it was keeping him afloat as the boat motored ahead.

## THIRTY-SIX

Shyla Benson had gotten little sleep since Hatch's surprise visit. Her mind replayed the words. I killed Graham. She didn't understand. None of it made sense. The Army had given her an explanation, but most of the details had been redacted for confidentiality purposes. A slap in the face. When the other members of her late husband's team had come to pay their respects, they too held back. The secrets of a brotherhood she never quite understood.

Hatch had dropped a bombshell, and in the blink of an eye had disappeared. Shyla knew Hatch through the stories Graham had shared. None of the things he'd said matched what she'd told her. There had to be more. She needed to know.

Shyla remembered the story of Pat Tillman, the legendary professional football player that joined the Army after 9/11. She also knew the tragedy of the friendly fire incident that ended his life. She wondered now if her husband had faced the same fate. War was an ugly thing. The damage it did to her Graham over the years of service had taken its toll. If Hatch was responsible, Shyla couldn't imagine the burden she'd been carrying.

The anger at first receiving Hatch's news had receded. Now she was left only with an empty sadness, a hole that could only be filled with the truth of that day.

Shyla now stood behind the wrap-around counter in her diner, preparing the day's ingredients. She had gotten herself and Maddie up around five AM to head to the diner early. The day was already looking dreary, what with the thunderstorm that had been outside since late the previous night. The forecast said it wouldn't get much better throughout the day.

She thought of her younger brother, Tyler. Shyla hadn't wanted to drag her daughter in this morning and had called him twice last night and once this morning, but he hadn't answered or bothered to call back. Maybe he was still with Hatch, she thought. Maybe the cell tower's signal had been knocked out from the storm.

Maddie sat at the counter in her usual seat. Shyla had poured a bowl of cereal for her daughter. The young girl had gotten a few bites in before slouching in her chair and letting her eyes drift closed. She kept jolting herself awake, then letting herself drift off again, before she decided talking might be the best cure. "Mommy," Maddie said. "How come people don't come in early to help you?"

Shyla sighed. "Because I run the restaurant, and I like to do the prepping."

"But I'm so tired," Maddie whined. "Why can't I stay home with Nana?"

"Nana needs more sleep than you do. And this afternoon when she picks you up, you can take a big nap when you guys get home. Does that sound good?"

"I don't like naps."

Shyla sighed again and continued her prep work. She was chopping onions on a wooden cutting board. "Sometimes you have to make sacrifices in life. Like getting up a little earlier to get your day started. To get ready for the rush, you know will approach." Putting down her knife, she looked at a photo of her late husband on the wall behind Maddie. She loved looking at the picture and seeing Graham's beautiful smile. He was the one who'd convinced her to open the diner before he'd passed away. Shyla felt that waking up early to get the restaurant up and running was a way of keeping Graham alive. At the very least, it was her way of honoring his memory.

Shyla's gaze drifted back to her daughter, still slouched in her chair and looking more bored than ever. "How about I make you some pancakes?"

Maddie perked up at the suggestion. "With chocolate chips and whipped cream?"

"You bet, kiddo."

"Yay!" Maddie rested her elbows on the table, balancing her cheeks between her palms to keep her head up.

Shyla grabbed a metal bowl from a cabinet and two eggs from the fridge behind her. As she turned back around, the trees outside stopped their rustling. An eerie calm took hold.

Tsunami sirens howled just as they had two days ago. The lights blinked on and off in rapid succession. Maddie screamed and covered her ears with her palms. In between panicked crying, she yelled, "I hate these stupid drills! Why would they be doing this now?"

Shyla patted her daughter's messy head of hair as she stepped out from behind the counter and approached the windows. A raging wave was fast approaching from the shore. It flowed through the streets like a whitewater river, knocking down telephone lines, trees, and small houses. Bursting through windows and doors like an army raiding an enemy town.

At this rate, Shyla had no time to board up the windows and doors. She looked at the evacuation map on the other side of the wall in a rush, determining the next best steps.

The siren sounded again.

Maddie started crying. "I wish Daddy was here," she said. "He'd know what to do."

A rush of emotion flooded Shyla in unison with the wave flooding everything else. She could be just as capable as her husband had been. But her daughter was right. He would have had a plan made up in the blink of an eye.

Grabbing the keys to her van from the counter, she was about to carry Maddie out the front door when the monster of water picked up the vehicle from the road and carried it into a lamp post. The car wrapped around the pole, and the inside was broken into by the rushing water crashing through the windshield and side windows and tossing the doors open.

Buildings collapsed closer to her location. The rushing water would come for the diner soon.

Shyla rushed back to Maddie and scooped her up.

She thought back to what Maddie had said about her father. *What would Graham do?*

The churning flood water was littered with debris as it rushed up to the diner, threatening to break through the windows. It reminded Shyla of the time they'd taken Maddie to the aquarium. It was the last time they'd all been together as a family. Graham had deployed the next day.

In the flash it took for that memory to appear, the water level had reached the height of the Help Wanted sign on the window directly in front of Shyla. An uprooted tree crashed through the glass, followed by the gush of pouring rain and salt water.

Shyla tossed Maddie over the counter and used the stool to clamor after her. The water chased them. They raced back through the kitchen. She looked up at the roof access. Seeking high ground was their best chance of survival. "Stay right behind me. We've got to climb."

Maddie was tight on her heels as Shyla shimmied up the ladder. Releasing the latch, she shoved her shoulder into the door. Just as the seal broke, a gust of wind forced it closed again. Shyla stepped higher, pressing her hunched back against it. Her legs strained as she forced open the hatchway.

It was halfway open when the rung she stood on snapped. Lack of use had rotted the wood. The heavy rectangular unit slammed the door shut as Shyla lost her footing and came careening back down the ladder. She caught herself before barreling into her daughter.

"We can't go up!" Shyla looked at the broken ladder. "We'll have to find another place to ride this out."

Maddie was crying uncontrollably now as she descended to the floor. Shyla dropped down, landing beside her daughter. Her heart raced as she watched the rising water fill the interior of the restaurant.

## THIRTY-SEVEN

The small town of Fairhaven, Oregon, had been pummeled by the floodwater. The giant wave was no longer, but a deep river still flowed through the streets. Boat was the only method of transportation until the flood drains could process all the saltwater.

People stood on top of their houses with their families. The only refuge they could get from the flooded streets and presumably their flooded homes. They held each other, some discussing their next steps and others crying or simply enjoying the warmth of their loved ones' embraces.

Banyan steered them through the watery streets. Lampposts had been knocked over. Thankfully, the power lines were underground, so they were safe there. Then again, it was only seven AM and no one's house lights were on.

Tyler grabbed his phone from his back pocket as a voicemail notification came in. Surprised to see it still worked, he thought it would've been damaged from getting drenched by the storm and tsunami wave. He immediately tried calling his sister. Straight to voicemail. Tried again. Nothing. Cell towers in the distance hadn't been knocked over, but maybe the power lines were damaged after all.

Looking at his phone, he cancelled the call. Then he realized the voicemail icon at the bottom of his screen had a circular red badge at the corner and a white number three in the middle. Clicking on it, he saw three missed messages from Shyla. He looked around at the group to see if they were paying attention elsewhere. Almost all of them had their eyes ahead. Except the Hatch woman.

"Everything alright?" she asked.

"Uh, yeah. Fine."

She leveled him a look that told him she wasn't convinced.

"I just missed a few calls from my sister." He held up his phone to show her the missed calls.

Hatch nodded in understanding and went back to observing the wreckage.

Tyler listened to the first message from Shyla. "Hey, Tyler. It's Shyla. I need your help with Maddie tomorrow morning. I know you've been, um, busy recently, but I'm hoping you can come through for me this time. Ok, call me back."

Then the second, about two hours later. "Tyler, I don't know where you are or what you're doing, but I wish you didn't ignore me like this. I'm really worried about you, and I need your help. If you can't come through for me, maybe I just won't call you again."

Finally, the third, around five AM. "You know what, I don't care anymore. I'll just go in early today and drag my tired five-year-old with me. I can't believe you'd rather gallivant around, doing some shady shit with shady people. I was trying to give you an out. An excuse to leave. But if you'd really rather be there, fine."

Tyler's heart sank into the pit of his stomach. Of course, he would have been there for his sister in a heartbeat. Or he would've at least called back if he'd have known. He kicked himself for getting involved in all of this. It was his fault the bomb had gone off. It had to be. If the bomb hadn't gone off, the tsunami wouldn't have happened, and Shyla and Maddie would be safe.

Tyler looked back in the direction of the diner, but they'd already passed it. While listening to the messages, he hadn't realized how close they were to where he'd buried Dibner.

"They should be safe. They're at the diner."

The Hatch woman placed a hand on his shoulder. "We'll find them." Hatch smiled. "I know a thing or two about missed phone calls from concerned loved ones. But I know she did whatever she could to keep herself and your niece safe." She placed a reassuring hand on Tyler's shoulder. "If she's half as tough as the man she married, then I'm sure she's okay."

Tyler nodded and filed the thought away in the back of his mind. The task right now was to find the man he'd buried.

Banyan steered the boat to almost the exact spot Tyler had parked his sister's van just two days ago. The grave would have been just a few yards in front of it. But he couldn't see it. The flood water had dissipated in this area, probably sinking into the ground and mingling with the dirt and vegetation.

Tyler dropped to his knees in the sloppy mud. He tore at the wet ground with his hands. "No, no. this can't be! It was here. I know it was."

The others moved around him, assisting in searching the area.

"The pipe. Where's the pipe?" His voice echoed off the surrounding trees. Pounding the wet earth, he cursed loud enough for all the world to hear. His tear-filled eyes searched the heavens for an answer. Not far off in the distance, he received it. His heart sank at the sight.

The PVC pipe with the elbow joint still attached was lodged in the twisted branches of a nearby tree.

Tyler brought his hands to the top of his head. He slapped his head in a violent fury. The thick mud coating his hands doing little to soften the blows. Tears fell freely. His life was over. He killed Frank Dibner. In cold blood. He left a man to die in the ground. There wasn't an attorney in Suzuki's arsenal capable of spinning that in his favor.

A wave of guilt crashed and piled on top of the lingering numbness surrounding the truth. He thought of his sister and niece and the wave his actions brought down on this shore and wondered if he had also been indirectly responsible for their deaths, too. His knees buckled.

A loud groan sounded over the wind and rain. In Tyler's state of disconnect, he thought it had come from him. Then he heard it again. He recognized the sound. He'd heard it before. On the night he buried Dibner. The screams of a dying man. They were haunting him now, but they were weaker now. He was losing his mind, the torment of his choices had already begun.

"What was that?" Hatch said. The group fell into a hush and looked around the tree-littered marsh.

In the midst of all the fallen trees and debris, they had their answer.

---

FRANK DIBNER WAS COVERED in mud, drenched to the bone from the rain, and flushed red from anger. He was shaking, probably from the cold, but that could have been from anger, too. The older man stuck a finger up and started running towards them.

"You!" he pointed at Tyler. The man ran toward him faster than Tyler had anticipated. Dibner launched himself onto Tyler. Grabbing him by the shirt collar, he placed his face mere inches away. "You." Spittle flew onto Tyler's cheeks as his heart beat faster.

Hatch and Banyan inserted themselves between the men, Hatch standing in front of Tyler and Banyan in front of Dibner. The older man continued to seethe with rage as Hatch spoke. "Let's all calm down. Stay rational."

Tyler wondered how she kept it together so well after losing her partner. He didn't know if they were a 'thing,' but he'd seen the look on Hatch's face when the man had sacrificed himself to save her life. All their lives.

"Stay rational?" Dibner struggled against Banyan's grip on his shoulders. "This man tried to kill me!"

Tyler spoke up. "You were there, man. Someone else was making me do it."

"You still did it!"

"And I tried to save you," Tyler said. "I put a pipe in there for you to breathe and maybe find your way out."

"I found my way out alright, no thanks to you."

"That's enough," Suzuki said, approaching Dibner. The other man cowered as Suzuki held his head high and steadied himself on his cane. "Tyler here got himself into some trouble, but he has done more than enough to make up for it. He did something awful to you, I realize that. But this boy wouldn't harm a fly if it were up to him. It was out of his control."

Dibner gave Tyler an unforgiving look, then took a moment to look around at the group, as if noticing everyone else for the first time. His vision had been tunneled in on Tyler for the last few minutes.

"Who are all these people, Yohei?" He looked over at Akira, standing behind her father. "Why is your daughter here? What happened?"

Suzuki gave Dibner a small rundown of the past day's events. The speech and press conference. The abduction. The transfer facility. Theo Clay, Parker Chase, and the bomb. The tsunami.

It exhausted Tyler to hear about all these things he'd just been through. He hadn't had time to process any of it until now.

A rescue boat approached them from a distance. They were about half-a-mile inland, following the same path Banyan had taken them on.

"Listen, Frank, this man here is losing a lot of blood." Suzuki gestured to the wounded guard. "Looks like we can get help from that boat."

Dibner nodded in agreement.

Suzuki looked around at the crowd of people on the boat. "I can't say this journey started on good terms, but I am now so grateful to you all. Thank you."

Everyone nodded and smiled in acknowledgement. Approaching Hatch, he grabbed her hands.

"I'm so sorry for what you had to go through back there. But I get the sense you've seen more than your fair share of death and experienced more pain than most. The warrior walks a path few dare. And we, who are born from the peace they provide, are forever in their debt."

Hatch softened and bowed her head. "It was a pleasure to meet you, Yohei Suzuki. Thank you."

He tightened his grip on her hands and then let go, replacing her hands with the cane he'd propped against the side of his leg.

Akira popped out from behind him and gave her new friend a big hug. Hatch crouched down and enveloped the girl in her embrace. "You were so brave today," Hatch said. "I know it may not seem like it, but this experience will allow you to see life through a completely different lens. Trust me."

Akira nodded and smiled, then ran back to her father.

The rescue boat pulled up alongside them. Three people of varying ages stood ready to retrieve any wounded. All wore heavy coats covered by rain ponchos. "You all need help?"

Suzuki piped up. "Just four of us. We've got a man losing a lot of blood."

"Hop on." Two of the passengers from the rescue boat moved onto Banyan's and lifted the guard over. The third passenger immediately began to apply pressure on the guard's wound.

Tyler approached the side of the boat and faced the rescuers. "Any idea what happened to the diner, Crackers?"

"That's in one of the areas that got hit pretty bad," the younger one said. "There's still a lot of people unaccounted for."

"Got it," Tyler replied. "Thanks." He hung his head in defeat. Max placed a hand on his arm and gave him a silent reassuring nod. It buoyed him, even if it was difficult to believe he'd ever see his sister again.

Dibner stepped onto the other boat, followed by Suzuki and Akira, and then they headed toward the medical facility.

"Let's get to that diner," Banyan said, turning the boat in the opposite direction of the rescuers. He looked back at Tyler as he continued to steer. "Time to find your family, kid."

As they rode through the devastated wasteland of the town he called home, Tyler said a silent prayer. Something he hadn't done in the years since Graham died. The only answer came in wind pushing the boat forward.

# THIRTY-EIGHT

Water encircled Shyla Benson's feet. It was rising by the second. The cold penetrated her jeans and pricked at her skin like a thousand tiny needles. The streets were a danger zone of hurtling debris, churned by the raging floodwater.

Maddie tugged at her arm. "Mommy, I'm scared."

"Me too, baby. Me too."

As she passed the back counter, Shyla snatched their jackets and a towel. Cold water licked at her heels as Shyla carried Maddie into the freezer and pulled the door latch down.

Inside, Shyla fought against rushing water to close it. With the latch secured, the water slowed.

But the gap at the bottom let water seep into an otherwise air-tight room. Feeling the water lap around her feet furthered her rage over the issue she'd noticed two months ago. That gap had cost her hundreds of dollars, and now it might literally be the death of her.

Without pausing for longer than it took to swear under her breath, she applied the only budget-friendly fix she'd been able to come up with since she'd discovered the gap. She wadded the towel at the base of the door.

Water continued to enter the space, this time in more of a trickle than the gush of before. Their own personal ice rink was forming at their feet. Shyla shivered as she put Maddie in her jacket. She zipped her daughter up and gave her shoulders a gentle rub before donning her own coat.

Shyla picked her daughter up and stood on a wooden crate at the side of the room. Maddie cried into her mother's shoulder. Shyla embraced her daughter tightly and brushed the little girl's hair with her hand. "It's okay baby. It'll all be okay."

The girl's sobs lessened as Shyla's deep breathing and gentle embrace calmed her. Maddie jolted her head up, almost knocking into Shyla's. Her eyes were wide with concern. "Where's Uncle Tyler?" she asked. "Is he okay?"

"I'm sure he'll be alright. We'll find him when this is all over."

Maddie rested her head on her mother's shoulder again. The sounds of rushing water dissipated outside the freezer door, and the trickle that had gotten through the freezer was slowing down even more.

"We're safe, sweetheart." Shyla placed her daughter down on the crate and stepped down to unlock the freezer. The latch wouldn't budge.

Her heart rate began to skyrocket. She looked for a knife or mallet or something to chip away at any ice. She found a wooden block and pounded away at the hinge. It had to have frozen over, she thought. In a panic, she gave up on beating the ice away and began to ram her shoulder into the door with all the force she could muster.

The door opened just enough for her to see that something was blocking the outside. A stainless-steel table from the back kitchen had washed up and landed right in front of the door, blocking her from opening it or getting out at all.

"What's happening, Mommy?"

"The door seems to be stuck, sweetie. It might take a little longer to get out of here, but I'll find a way."

Maddie nodded and hugged her knees to her chest and wrapped her arms around them, burying her chin in her knees and staring intently at her mother.

Shyla's energy stores were draining fast from the wet feeling on her feet and the coldness enveloping her from the outside. A gust of wind tore through them. The door slammed shut, shaking the walls.

There was no way the situation could have gotten worse. Or so she thought.

Then the power went out, and she couldn't see anything past the darkness.

---

HATCH, Banyan, Tyler, and Max navigated back into town. The flooding had dissipated, and the rain had stopped completely. Mild wind blew in a steady stream against their faces, drying any water from the storm and waves. The water level lowered to a point, rendering the boat useless.

"This is as far as we can take her," Banyan said as he cut the motor. The boat glided to a stop, running aground and coming to rest against an overturned dumpster blocking the street.

They disembarked and began traversing the next few blocks to the diner by foot. The water was knee high. The bitter cold stung at her legs, but Hatch barely registered it. Her mind was focused on one thing and one thing only: finding Tyler's family.

The damage came clearly into view now that the rain and flood weren't obscuring any details. Most of the buildings had damaged windows and soaked interiors. Law enforcement and rescue squads talked to the townsfolk outside their houses and assessed the damage done. They worked on evacuating anyone in the area with as many belongings as they could find. These people needed to find food, water, and shelter until long-term arrangements could be made. Hatch had seen it before, the despondent vacant stares. She'd seen it on foreign soil, in the faces of those displaced by war.

She remembered the faces of the men she'd seen outside the pool in Coronado. The warrior path preparing their mind for times like this. In that moment, she thought of the one SEAL who'd paid the ultimate price so that she could keep moving forward. And so she did. Move forward. One icy step at a time.

Tyler walked alongside Hatch, with Max on his other side, stroking his arm. Banyan walked behind the trio. Tyler's head hung low as he kept shaking it and muttering to himself.

Hatch looked over at the young man and tried to meet his eyes while they walked. "Hey, none of this is your fault." Her words got his attention. "In all honesty, I thought it was mine, too."

"How could any of it have been your fault? I was the one who drove the van to abduct the Suzuki's in the first place."

"It doesn't matter at this point," Hatch said. "Everything that's happened is now in the past. There's nowhere to move but forward."

"How?" Tyler sighed. "Forward just seems bleak and hopeless."

"Ever heard the phrase, darkest before the dawn?"

Tyler nodded. He stumbled on something in the murky water and caught himself on a nearby stop sign bent at an angle.

"This is one of those times."

"I don't feel like the sun will ever rise again. Not for me. Not after this." Tyler's voice was hollow.

"Sometimes you have to fail to go forward. But trust me when I say this, the hardness of your challenge tests the truest resolve of your character."

"Another life lesson?"

Hatch nodded. "Taught by one of my greatest teachers. Your brother-in-law."

Tyler stopped in his tracks. "And what does the fearless Hatch know about failure?"

She turned away from him. "I failed to bring your brother-in-law home."

Silence ensued as they continued their walk forward. Then Tyler spoke again,, a little quieter. "He always said if there was anyone who could make sure he came back alive, it was you."

Hatch blinked for a second longer than normal. Her heart wrenched at the words. She tried to think of something, anything, to make it up to the young man beside her.

Before she could respond, Tyler continued. "After seeing what you did on that platform back there, I agree with him."

"But I didn't bring him back."

"Then no one else could have, either."

They exchanged amicable glances as they reached the outside of the restaurant.

A large tree had blown through the front window, right next to the Help Wanted sign. The inside had been ravaged by the storm and flood.

"Where's her van?" Tyler asked, looking around the parking lot in a panic. Then he turned back to the window. Everyone scanned the interior as much as they could see past the tree and through the other windows.

Tyler picked his phone back out of his pocket. No calls from Shyla. He tried to call her again. He shook his head. "Nothing."

Hatch turned her attention back to the parking lot. If it was a utility van, it couldn't have gone far, even with natural forces taking it away. Out of the corner of her eye, she spotted a white vehicle flipped over on its roof.

She bolted from the restaurant and to the overturned vehicle. Tyler and Banyan searched the streets and other nearby buildings for Shyla and Maddie. Maybe they'd fled on foot after the storm. They weren't in the vehicle. Had they gone out into the flood and washed away? Hatch's heart lurched at the thought of having to recover their bodies.

Hatch left the van to search the streets. But something wasn't right. Shyla wouldn't have taken her young daughter out into a raging storm with tsunami sirens blaring. Hatch turned back to the vehicle. The entire side was dented, as if it had wrapped around something. Maybe it had. She peered into the driver's side window one more time.

No key in the ignition.

Shyla and Maddie couldn't have gotten back in the car after the tsunami swept through.

Hatch's gut led her back to the restaurant.

"Where are you going?" Banyan asked. "They could be anywhere out here. We have to find them."

"I don't think they're out there," Hatch replied, stepping through the broken floor-to-ceiling window, just scraping by the tree lying through it. The rest of the group ran back to her and followed her in.

The restaurant had an open floor plan of sorts, so she could see most of the interior in one quick scan. No sign of them. No sign of life.

That couldn't be it. She headed over to the counter and back through the kitchen. A large stainless-steel table had wedged itself in the middle of the back hallway, blocking the freezer room door. She grabbed hold of a leg and tried to move it free, but it wouldn't budge. Tyler and Banyan had followed her in while Max continued to search the area outside. The trauma of the night and the death of her brother were evident in every step.

Hatch banged on the freezer door. No answer. "Help me move this out of the way, I want to check the freezer."

"Why would they be in the freezer?" Tyler asked.

"To seal out any flood water that might have gone through the rest of the restaurant," Hatch said. "It's where Graham would have gone."

Tyler and Banyan helped Hatch push the table forward and out of the door's opening enough to stand directly in front of it. The door was stuck. Frozen water at the base sealing it closed. "Give me a hand. It won't budge."

Hatch pulled on the handle while Tyler and Banyan used kitchen knives found on the floor to chip away at the ice.

After several minutes of struggling, the hinge squeaked, and a loud cracking sound filled the air as Hatch freed the door from the clutches of the icy ground.

The door swung open. Tyler was the first to enter the freezer. "No!" His words hung on the plume of crystalized air.

Hatch followed him inside. Inside were Shyla and Maddie, huddled together. Neither moved. And for a moment, neither did anyone else.

---

THE TWO WERE CURLED on a crate at the side of the room. Their faces a ghostly white with lips a soft blue. Shyla had her daughter wrapped in her coat. They'd had to be frozen in there for at least an hour. Hatch couldn't bear to witness another sacrifice. Too much had been given already.

The woman and small girl looked as good as dead.

Tyler rushed in and hugged his sister and niece in his arms, letting tears flow down his cheeks. "Please, God, no!"

Hatch and Banyan moved past him and immediately began checking for a pulse. Hatch felt the icy skin of Shyla, running her index and middle finger along the carotid artery while Tyler shuddered in agonizing grief. And then she felt it. A pulse, faint, but there. "She's alive."

Hatch shot a glance at Banyan who was still holding a finger to the small girl's neck. A teardrop, frozen in place on the right side of her cheek, glistened like a diamond. In what felt like a thousand lifetimes, Banyan finally gave her the answer she'd been waiting for. It came in the form of a long-relieved exhale. "Good to go."

"We've got to get them warm. And fast." Hatch moved Tyler aside and then began stripping off her wetsuit. "Skin on skin contact is the fastest way to stave off hypothermia."

Shyla blinked her eyes open and moved her head to look at Hatch just as her body convulsed violently. Her breaths were labored, and puffs of cool air rose from her mouth. "Hatch," was the only word she could get out, and Hatch almost didn't hear it.

"Let's get them out of here," Hatch said as she handed the wetsuit to Tyler. Banyan was already lifting Maddie and making his way to the open door.

Hatch pulled her shirt over Shyla's head, sealing them both inside. Her skin pressed against the icy flesh of Graham's widow. She absorbed the cold, exchanging it for her own warmth.

Tyler followed Hatch's lead and did the same thing with his niece. Tears continued to fall from the young man's face.

Banyan was already on the phone with Tracy, working on getting them the fastest extraction possible. Tracy, fearing the worst, had already taken to the air and was hovering over Fairhaven in a helicopter he'd commandeered prior to the tsunami's landfall.

After a few minutes, the little girl blinked her eyes open. The icy diamond fell from her cheek as she looked up at the young man holding her. "Uncle Tyler?"

He smiled down at his niece and smiled. "I'm right here," he said.

Maddie buried her face in his chest as she welcomed Tyler's warm embrace.

"Can you wiggle your toes? Your fingers?" Banyan asked Shyla.

She responded by making small movements with her feet and hands.

Eventually, she had defrosted enough to take in the scene in front of her. Tears formed in her eyes as she saw her brother with her daughter. She looked up at Hatch. "Thank you," she said. "How can I ever repay you?"

The words struck Hatch. This woman, who she'd taken so much from, felt the need to repay her. "I owe your family a debt I could never repay. Not in a thousand lifetimes."

Hatch crouched down and took the woman's nearly frozen hand into her palms. She looked toward the help wanted sign hanging from a broken chunk of glass still attached to the frame. Taking in the devastation caused by the wave, Hatch said to Shyla, "Looks like you could use an extra hand around here. Mind if I stick around for a bit?"

Shyla's answer came in the form of a weak smile. In seeing it, Hatch felt the first inkling of hope since Cruise had entered the dark water.

# THIRTY-NINE

*A tsunami hit the coast of Fairhaven, Oregon, this morning. Despite extensive damage to the whole town, no casualties have been reported. However, oil conglomerate executive Theo Clay and his personal security have been reported missing. As a result, Aurora Nuclear's CEO, Yohei Suzuki, met with the regulatory committee, and a decision has been made to postpone the opening of the reinstated offshore nuclear facility until further notice...*

Hatch sat in the fluorescent-lit hospital waiting room. More patients than normal swarmed the halls. Families huddled together in their rooms, praying and allowing themselves to doze off while they awaited the status of their relatives.

Hatch and Banyan had loaded Shyla and Maddie onto a shuttle after finding them nearly frozen in the diner's freezer room. Hatch watched the news report about the entire event she'd witnessed herself that morning, grateful to hear no one else had died from it. Cruise's sacrifice had saved lives. Rebuilding the town of Fairhaven would take months. Rebuilding herself would take a lifetime. But helping Shyla get back on her feet would be the beginning. She felt in helping her get the diner back in order, Hatch would be, in some small way, honoring Cruise's dream.

Banyan returned to the room, taking the seat next to Hatch. He'd walked outside to answer a call from Jordan Tracy. "Talon can have the jet ready and waiting within the hour."

Hatch ran her fingers along her scarred arm, contemplating. This entire operation had gone wrong because of one small hesitation. It had cost Cruise his life, and while the bomb would have gone off anyway, she wasn't sure this was the path she wanted to be on anymore. Cruise had said he wanted to retire from the game after this op. Maybe it was time for her to do the same. "I'm not going back."

"Why not?" Banyan asked. "You're one of the best operators I've ever known."

"Thanks." Hatch smiled, still looking down at her arm. "It just feels like it's time for me to leave. Or at least, time to head out on my own path again." She faced Banyan and looked into his eyes. "You know Cruise felt that way too? Said he wanted to retire. Open a diner with me."

Banyan took on a pained expression as he remembered one of his best friends who was now waterborne. Then he smiled at the memory of Cruise. "That sounds like him. Never letting anyone know his decision until he's set on it, ready to put it into action. I guess he was waiting until the operation was finished."

Hatch nodded. "He was. I'm still kicking myself for leaving him hanging. When he asked me to go with him, I said, 'Let's just focus on the op.' The true answer in my gut was no. But maybe fear just had such a chokehold on me. Maybe I should have done the thing that scared me and said yes. Maybe he'd still be alive if I had."

"We can't think like that," Banyan said. "I like to think everything happens for a reason. This situation turned out the way it did for a reason." He looked away. "That's what I tell myself, anyway. Makes it hurt a little less. But I don't want you to blame yourself for the sacrifice Cruise made. I will miss my friend, but he determined his own fate and did what he thought was best for everyone else." Banyan sighed. "He was such a great man. But I almost wish he'd been selfish if it meant he'd still be here. I guess that makes me selfish."

Hatch took Banyan's hand in hers and squeezed. "If it weren't for your Swim Buddy, we all would have died," she said. "The tether system broke in a fluke accident, but the Swim Buddy still worked, and Cruise wouldn't have been able to swim out the second bomb otherwise. We'd have been stranded, and you'd have reached us right before the structure would have blown. You'd have been dead too."

Banyan gave a sad smile and looked her way again. "Thanks, Hatch."

"And I think he'd want me to tell you," Hatch continued, "before he stepped into the water, he declared he'd be waterborne until he returned. I thought you'd want to know that."

Banyan chuckled. "Classic parting words. Thanks for telling me."

"You're welcome."

"Listen Hatch, I know you tend to drift wherever the wind blows, but you don't have to disappear on me alright? I consider us friends, and it's important to have people to lean on. If you choose to accept it. I've already lost one buddy today. I don't need to lose another."

Hatch chuckled. "Alright. I accept that. The same goes for you."

Banyan nodded. "I better get going." He stood from his seat. "Always a pleasure working with you."

She stood from her seat and shook his hand. "Be safe out there."

Banyan nodded again and headed out of the waiting room door just as Shyla came into the room from the back hallway. "Thanks again for your help, Hatch. It means a lot."

"That's what I do."

"How long are you sticking around for?"

"Depends. The right time to leave usually presents itself before I can plan for it. I want to be here long enough to at least see you back on your feet again."

Shyla smiled and rubbed a hand on Hatch's upper back. A friendly gesture. Hatch wasn't used to that.

Maddie came bounding into the room and crashed into her mother with a big hug. Shyla almost fell over from the force. The doctor followed the young girl in, smiling at the child's enthusiasm. "Maddie did so well. She's all good to go."

"Thank you," Shyla said. Then she knelt down to eye level with her daughter, pushing the young girl's hair out of her face. "Sweetie, Hatch here is going to stay for a little while longer. What do you think?"

Maddie's eyes lit up as she screamed, "Yay!" And gave Hatch the same full-force hug.

Shyla smiled at the interaction as Hatch knelt down to embrace the girl. Maddie let go, still giddy with excitement, as she turned back to hug her mother's leg.

Hatch stood and turned more serious. "I think I owe you a conclusion to the story I was trying to tell the other night."

Shyla placed a gentle hand on Hatch's shoulder. "I think we'll have plenty of time to get to that."

# FORTY

Hatch crouched in front of the freezer door, attaching the new flap to the bottom. The door had a gap that allowed gushes of water to spill in, while Shyla and Maddie had tried to make a haven out of the small frozen room during the tsunami.

As Hatch put on the final piece to the cover, Shyla entered the narrow hallway.

Hatch stood to greet her, wiping her hands together as if removing any invisible dirt caked on her palms. "All finished."

"Thanks so much. You've been such a helping hand around here." Shyla wrapped an arm around the other woman and led her toward the front.

"It's been a great break from everything," Hatch said, feeling welcome in Shyla's embrace. "I thought I could go my whole life without needing anyone, or anything. I thought I could just get by on my own and worry about myself. In the last few months, I've learned how wrong I was. I think I needed you as much as you needed me. And I've come to accept that I might need others as well."

Shyla tilted the side of her head onto Hatch's and gripped her shoulder tighter.

Hatch had stayed in Fairhaven with Shyla, Tyler, their mother, and Maddie. They had an extra bed for her to sleep in and welcomed her company. Throughout the few months she was there, Hatch had spent time in solitude when she'd needed it, and time with the Pierce-Bensons when she didn't. She'd decided to pull her uncomfortable feelings to the forefront. While she wished things could have gone differently for her and Cruise, what Banyan had said to her resonated. It happened the way it had for a reason. Nothing could change that. So, Hatch thought the best way to honor Cruise in loving memory was to help Shyla get her diner reopened in the past few months following the tsunami.

Shyla let go of Hatch's shoulders and faced her. "I've really come to know you over these past few months. And we've already talked about it in full, but I just want to stress again that I know you've really beat yourself up for what happened to Graham." The women looked at Maddie drawing at the counter in front of them, oblivious to their conversation. "Maybe you don't need to hear this from me. But in case you do, I just want you to remember that your hesitation was completely human. I can't imagine the choice you had to make and the situation you were forced to live with. You have to forgive yourself for trusting your judgment."

Hatch nodded.

"Tyler told me about that day. When they abducted Yohei Suzuki and his daughter. He told me how he was in the driver's seat, and you had your gun pointed at him." Tyler sat an elderly couple in a booth on the other side of the restaurant. Looking back at the two women, he smiled. "But you didn't shoot." Shyla looked Hatch in the eyes, her own twinkling like a glass mirror. "Your hesitation saved my brother's life. And gave me a second shot at having my family around. Thank you so much."

The woman pulled Hatch into a gentle hug.

Behind them, the restaurant bustled with more patrons as Max and Tyler continued seating the guests and taking their orders. Hatch was proud to have been a part of revamping the establishment and also getting to know the family of Graham Benson a little better. She was finally ready to make peace with the past. That also meant making peace in the present and recognizing her deep desire to move on. She felt herself pulled away by something intangible. The 'itch' had resurfaced.

Hatch was surprised out of her thoughts as Maddie inserted herself between the women, joining in on the embrace. Her wrist brushed Hatch's scarred arm. Hatch noticed the girl wore the bracelet Graham had worn when he died. She was happy to see Maddie keeping her father alive in that way.

Hatch let go of the embrace and crouched down to Maddie's eye level. "When you're old enough to hear them, I have a million stories about your dad to tell you. He was one of the best friends I've ever had."

Maddie giggled and continued hugging her mother.

Hatch looked out the front window, the one the tree had blown through during the tsunami. In the distance, she could make out the tiny block of water where the nuclear transfer facility would have been. Cruise's body had never been recovered. She breathed in the salty air. Caught his scent, as she always did, carried now by the windswept sea where he would forever be.

She thought of the sacrifice he made for her and everybody else on that night. Hatch knew the best way to honor it was to keep going forward. Each step the living take, honors the dead who have gone before.

Finally, she'd forgiven herself for that day, too. Hatch would miss the man forever, but she knew in her heart that they wouldn't have stayed together if he'd made it back. Cruise had confirmed it himself. They both knew her heart belonged elsewhere.

*Savage.*

Savage had called a few times, but Hatch had never gotten back to him. She needed to clear her head and see where her heart landed.

Now she knew. There was only one stop left in her journey.

Shyla's voice chimed in, jerking Hatch out of her thoughts. "I hope you'll stick around now that the diner's up and running again. I'd hate to lose your help. But I understand if it may be time for you to move on now that I'm on my feet again."

Hatch met the woman with a sad smile. "Yeah...I think it's time for me to get going." She glanced at Tyler and Max. "But it seems like you're in good hands now."

Shyla smiled and pulled Hatch into a warm embrace again. "Thank you so much. Really."

Hatch nodded and pulled away, mussing Maddie's hair and leaving the counter.

On his way over from a table, Tyler pulled Hatch aside. "Are you leaving?"

"Yeah. Just feels like time."

Tyler nodded. "It's been really great to know you. Having you around has helped me feel more connected to my brother-in-law."

"How are things going between you and Max? I see you guys have been spending a lot of time together lately."

"The generous donation from Suzuki got her mother the treatment she needed. That's been a big help in Max's recovery too. There's a lot of work ahead, but someone once told me a challenge's difficulty is the truest test of character." He offered a smile. "And so, I'm working hard to honor that."

"Looks to me like you're doing a pretty good job of it."

"Thanks. And thanks for giving me a chance to make things right with my family. I owe you."

"You owe me nothing. I'm just glad everything worked out how it was supposed to." Hatch smiled and patted the young man on the shoulder, heading out of the diner for the last time.

Taking one last glimpse at the glistening oceanfront, she thought of Cruise. It was time to leave. She thought of the last thing he'd said to her. *I'm waterborne, until I return.* A tear ran down her cheek. He's home now.

# FORTY-ONE

Hatch arrived in Hawk's Landing in the mid-afternoon. The sun was shining brightly, and there wasn't a cloud in the sky. It was a big atmospheric shift from the cloudy, rainy, stormy days in Fairhaven. She'd been on the road for about five days now, including the nights she'd stopped at motels to sleep.

Now driving through her hometown toward her mother's house, Hatch recalled just how long it'd been since she'd been home last. Or rather, how much had happened since the organization she'd recently joined had tried to kill her and her family. It hadn't been nearly as long as it had when she'd joined the military and hadn't returned home for fifteen years.

Passing through the intersection where she'd almost been killed all that time ago brought with it a sea of other memories Hatch wished she could forget. Her drive took her past the lake where her sister's body had been found. This town now carried as much pain for Hatch as any battlefield she'd ever walked.

Aside from the brutal instances that occurred here, the town hadn't changed much. From the outside, anyway.

Hatch eventually turned onto the long dirt driveway that led to her childhood home. She saw the stone next to the mailbox that had her and her sister's childhood handprints painted on it.

Hatch and her sister were six years old. Both their mother and father were home, and they'd taken the girls outside to find a big enough rock. Then they took out the girls' favorite colors of paint and squirted it onto two plates. One for Hatch, the other for her sister. Each placed a hand on a plate and then, with the help of their parents, pressed their hand onto the stone to make a colorful, memorable mark. Then the girls proceeded to tackle each other and get paint everywhere. Their clothes, hair, and skin were stained for days. It was one of the few memories that still brought her joy.

Smiling at the memory, Hatch pulled in close to the house. Jed Russell's pickup truck sat at the front of the driveway. Jake was on the lawn a few yards away, practicing his karate with the makiwara board she'd made for him before the fire. He didn't have to wear his full uniform when practicing on his own, so he'd chosen to wear a t-shirt, his karate gi pants, and a black belt. Hatch felt a surge of pride in her nephew. He'd gotten his black belt since she'd been away.

Hatch got out of the car, the slam of the door getting Jake's attention. Turning around, he sprinted for her when he realized who she was. She almost crashed into the side of her car with the boy's impact, welcoming his embrace. Hatch thought it funny that when she'd met young Jake after his mother died, he'd been so aloof and reserved with her. It made Hatch happy to see she'd been able to get through the boy's walls.

Only a few seconds passed before Daphne squealed by the front door and ran down to greet her aunt, giving another tackling hug, though Jake's presence stabilized Hatch when Daphne launched herself at them. Hatch realized then just how much she'd missed her niece and nephew. During her travels, she'd thought of them often, waiting until the day she could see them again. Waiting until the day it was safe to return home.

In that moment, Hatch found what she'd been missing for a long time. Pure, unconditional love. Holding the children tightly in her arms, she kissed the tops of their heads.

When Hatch looked up, she saw her mother and Jed standing in the doorway, smiling at the scene in front of them.

All at once, Daphne and Jake broke out of their tight squeezing and began to ramble at Hatch over one another, each talking louder and louder to get their words noticed. Daphne talked a mile a minute about needing to show Hatch her paintings. Jake recounted his karate journey and receiving a black belt. Hatch had to swivel her head back and forth to catch the gist of what each child wanted to tell her. Squeezing them at her sides by their shoulders, she began walking with them up to the front door. "You guys will both have to show me what you've been up to. I've missed you so much."

"We missed you too, Auntie Rachel," Daphne squealed.

"I'm so happy you're back," Jake said.

As they climbed the porch steps, Hatch's mother stepped toward the pack in the doorframe. "We're all happy you're back," Jasmine said, pulling her daughter away from the kids and into a warm hug.

This was an unfamiliar experience for Hatch. She'd never hugged this much in a day, she was sure, but also by her mother? It seemed that even though she'd been away for a long time, Jasmine and Hatch's relationship continued to evolve. For that, Hatch was grateful.

"Let's go inside. We've got dinner cooking." Jasmine led the way following Jed.

The house was only a little different than Hatch remembered. The flooring had been replaced, the walls repainted, the kitchen and bathrooms renovated. "I like what you've done with the place."

"Thanks," Jed responded. "All my handy work."

"Nice job." Hatch liked the idea of change. Keeping the same roots and foundation, the same structure, but being able to change what was inside was important.

"What have you been up to, Aunt Rachel?" Daphne asked, taking a seat at the dinner table. Jake ran around the kitchen, getting plates and silverware.

Jed returned to his post at the stove. The aromas of onion, Worcestershire sauce, and garlic wafted around the room, making Hatch's mouth water.

Hatch was stuck on how to respond. Thinking it wasn't appropriate to describe all her adventures since she'd been gone, what with handling cartels, trafficking, and serial killers, she could at least say where she'd been. "I've done a lot of traveling. Went to Arizona, California, even Mexico for a little while. Then I ended up working with a team in Alaska and Oregon."

"Did you hear about the tsunami on the coast?" Jasmine asked. "Sounded like a real tragedy."

"I'll never forget it," Hatch said.

Jasmine leveled her daughter with a look, but when Hatch leveled her mother with the same in return, the older woman didn't pry. Jasmine cleared her throat and asked, "How long are you staying?"

Hatch's gut told her what it always did when someone asked her that. "Until it's time for me to go."

Jasmine rolled her eyes.

"Speaking of which, I've got another stop to make."

"What?" Jasmine put her hands on her hips and sighed. "You just got here."

Hatch laughed. "I'll be back for dinner. I promise. I just want to catch up with Savage. It's been a while. Long road back."

Jasmine and Jed exchanged a wide-eyed look. Her eyes betraying the worry they held. "It may have been too long, Rachel."

# FORTY-TWO

Hatch had heard her mother's remark before leaving for Dalton Savage's house, but refused to think anything of it. Ready to see him, if he wasn't ready to see her too, so be it.

Savage lived isolated by the woodland. It was peaceful, and probably tactical, given the man's line of work. He was no stranger to making enemies.

Hatch drove into the gravel driveway and put the vehicle in park at the corner of the sheriff's house. Giddy with anticipation, a feeling she was not used to. Having experienced a lot of foreign feelings in the last few months, now, she was starting to like it. Suppressing the sudden urge to leap out of the car and sprint toward the house, deciding she would look and feel psychotic doing so, she thought it appropriate to take a combat breath—two in, one out—and exit the vehicle calmly.

Not wanting to give herself away all at once, it was hard to contain the passion and excitement she felt. These she'd held on to for so long and shoved down for much longer. And they were finally bubbling to the surface, ready to come out. Her heart belonged to Savage. She was ready to accept that and let him know.

A pang of guilt hit her. Since Cruise's death, Hatch had come to terms with many things. One being that Cruise had loved her and she'd loved him too, but her connection to him was different than hers to Savage. This wasn't how she wanted to feel, given that Cruise had sacrificed his life for her. But she knew that more than anything else, Cruise would want her to be happy.

And now she could allow herself to be.

Hatch exhaled and knocked on the door. Her heart felt as though it would beat out of her chest. Palms sweating, she suddenly felt overheated in her clothes. Feeling her cheeks flushing, she had no doubt he'd be able to see it like a bright red tomato in the middle of a highway compared to her usual pale tone. Placing her palms to her warm cheeks, she tried to cool them off before Savage noticed.

Feet shuffled behind the door, then it opened.

"Can I help you?" A woman's voice sounded behind the slight opening. Hatch couldn't see all the way inside, let alone make out the figure in front of her. She only saw a sliver of the woman.

"Sorry, I thought Dalton Savage lived here. Maybe I have the wrong address?"

As Hatch turned to walk away, the woman opened the door more. "Oh, he lives here." She smiled. "Can I tell him who's here?"

"Rachel Hatch."

The woman's smile dropped as if it'd been slapped off her face. She tried to put it back on as though she hadn't lost it in the first place. "I've heard so much about you." Her tone didn't reassure Hatch that what she'd heard had been any good. As she turned to call for Savage, the woman rubbed her pregnant belly.

Hatch recognized the sight in front of her. The woman couldn't have been more than five months along. Not big, but definitely carrying.

"I'll be right back." Giving Hatch another tight-lipped smile, she left the door open while she went to grab Savage.

Hatch bolted for the car. Of course he'd developed a relationship with a beautiful woman and gotten her pregnant. What was Hatch thinking, that he'd wait around for her forever? She'd taken over half a year to 'clear her mind' and 'figure out her thoughts' when she'd known in her gut all along and could have said yes when she'd seen him in Kentucky.

Of course, she'd waited too long, and she was too late. Her hesitation, once again, cost her more than she could stand to bear.

On the way to her car, she heard Savage's voice call after her from the house. She continued walking, almost jogging, keeping her head down so he wouldn't see her.

The front door shut, and she heard him running after her. She sped up.

Hatch had reached her car by the time Savage caught up to her. She felt his presence right behind her, but still yanked the door handle. He proceeded to shut it before she could open it all the way. He was standing close to her now, his hand still on the door. Hatch held her face away from him, embarrassed at even being here. Holding back tears, she refused to unleash them in front of him.

But they started coming anyway. Hatch was so confused. When Cruise had walked away for the last time, she'd cried. And now she was crying again? Over another man?

Who was she?

Savage took her chin in a gentle hand and tilted her face to look at his. She didn't make eye contact as a single tear streamed down her cheek. Out of the corner of her eye, she saw Savage's face soften. His eyebrows tilted down, and he gripped her soul in his gaze.

He pulled Hatch into a tight hug. For a moment, she hugged him back fiercely, never wanting to let go. In the next, she pushed him away.

"I don't understand," she said, still avoiding his eyes.

"I didn't hear from you at all." Savage held Hatch's shoulders in his hands. "You left me with no answer in Kentucky or in the months following." He sighed. "I met Becca not long after. She supported me, and we fell in love."

Hatch felt her heart shattering into a million pieces as Savage's verbal knife twisted the shards of glass. But he was right. Purposely she hadn't contacted him. Thinking she was sorting out her thoughts, but really, Hatch had just let them spiral out of control until she couldn't handle it anymore.

Just when Hatch had thought she was through with avoidance and hesitation, here she was reaping the last of its rewards.

Wiping away the few tears she'd allow to fall, Hatch looked into his eyes. "Are you happy?"

"Yes... am."

Hatch smiled. "That's all that matters then." Gripping the door handle again, she began to gently pull.

Savage looked back at his home, and Hatch followed his gaze. Becca was standing in the window giving a reassuring smile and nod before disappearing behind the sheer curtain and retreating further into the house.

"I am so sorry." Savage shook his head. "If it's any consolation, I did want to wait forever."

"It would have been unfair to expect that of you. Besides, we'll always have that kiss."

Savage smiled and stepped away from the car, but he said nothing.

As Hatch got in, she said, "Watch your six."

"You too. Where are you off to now?"

"I told my mom I'd be home for dinner. After that, I'm not sure. Somewhere between anywhere and nowhere."

She shut the door, and Savage nodded his goodbye. He waited to head into the house until she pulled out of his driveway.

After getting on the road, her phone rang on the passenger seat. The ID spelled out Jordan Tracy's name. Hatch answered and heard his voice. "Hatch, it's been a while. Just checking in. I heard you left Fairhaven on your own."

"You're spying on me now?"

Tracy chuckled on the other end. "Just keeping tabs on one of our best."

Hatch marveled at the irony. The company that tried to kill her, then recruited her, and was now checking in on her, was the biggest pill of irony she'd ever swallowed. But deep down, she was glad Tracy had called.

Tracy spoke again. "So, you've had a couple months to think things over. Have you decided whether you want to stay on board?"

Hatch thought for a moment longer. Deciding that when someone wanted an answer, she would give it to them right then and there. She owed it, not just to them, but to herself to make her decisions when she felt them in her gut.

Her fingers ran across the words of the tattoo she'd gotten all those years ago. Now covered by the twisted scar extending along her arm, she could still read the words as if it were the day she'd had them etched permanently into her flesh. They never rang truer than they did right now.

*It's no use going back to the past. Because I was a different person then.*

"I'm still in, but under one condition." She looked out the rearview mirror at the sunset behind her. "I work alone."

"Done. We don't have anything for you right now, but I'll call you as soon as we get something. What'll you do until then?"

"I don't know. I think I'll just drift for a while."

---

**Rachel Hatch returns in *Fastrope*.**

*Hatch closed a major chapter in her life. Drifting between everywhere and nowhere, she seeks to find her new path. Like any pathfinder, Hatch cuts through the pain of her past by one step at a time.*

**ORDER NOW:**
https://www.amazon.com/gp/product/B0BHZLQHF4

Join the LT Ryan reader family & receive a free copy of the Rachel Hatch story, *Fractured*. Click the link below to get started: https://ltryan.com/rachel-hatch-newsletter-signup-1

GET your very own Rachel Hatch merchandise today! Click the link below to find coffee mugs, t-shirts, and even signed copies of your favorite L.T. Ryan thrillers! https://ltryan.ink/EvG_

# THE RACHEL HATCH SERIES

Drift

Downburst

Fever Burn

Smoke Signal

Firewalk

Whitewater

Aftershock

Whirlwind

Tsunami

Fastrope

*Sidewinder (Coming Soon)*

## RACHEL HATCH SHORT STORIES

Fractured

Proving Ground

The Gauntlet

Join the LT Ryan reader family & receive a free copy of the Rachel Hatch story, Fractured. Click the link below to get started:

https://ltryan.com/rachel-hatch-newsletter-signup-1

Get your very own Rachel Hatch merchandise today! Click the link below to find coffee mugs, t-shirts, and even signed copies of your favorite L.T. Ryan thrillers! https://ltryan.ink/EvG_

# ALSO BY L.T. RYAN

**Find All of L.T. Ryan's Books on Amazon Today!**

### The Jack Noble Series

*The Recruit (free)*

*The First Deception (Prequel 1)*

*Noble Beginnings*

*A Deadly Distance*

*Ripple Effect (Bear Logan)*

*Thin Line*

*Noble Intentions*

*When Dead in Greece*

*Noble Retribution*

*Noble Betrayal*

*Never Go Home*

*Beyond Betrayal (Clarissa Abbot)*

*Noble Judgment*

*Never Cry Mercy*

*Deadline*

*End Game*

*Noble Ultimatum*

*Noble Legend*

*Noble Revenge*

*Never Look Back (Coming Soon)*

## Bear Logan Series

*Ripple Effect*

*Blowback*

*Take Down*

*Deep State*

## Bear & Mandy Logan Series

*Close to Home*

*Under the Surface*

*The Last Stop*

*Over the Edge*

*Between the Lies (Coming Soon)*

## Rachel Hatch Series

*Drift*

*Downburst*

*Fever Burn*

*Smoke Signal*

*Firewalk*

*Whitewater*

*Aftershock*

*Whirlwind*

*Tsunami*

*Fastrope*

*Sidewinder (Coming Soon)*

## Mitch Tanner Series

*The Depth of Darkness*

*Into The Darkness*

*Deliver Us From Darkness*

## Cassie Quinn Series

*Path of Bones*

*Whisper of Bones*

*Symphony of Bones*

*Etched in Shadow*

*Concealed in Shadow*

*Betrayed in Shadow*

*Born from Ashes*

## Blake Brier Series

*Unmasked*

*Unleashed*

*Uncharted*

*Drawpoint*

*Contrail*

*Detachment*

*Clear*

*Quarry (Coming Soon)*

**Dalton Savage Series**

*Savage Grounds*

*Scorched Earth*

*Cold Sky*

*The Frost Killer (Coming Soon)*

**Maddie Castle Series**

*The Handler*

*Tracking Justice*

*Hunting Grounds (Coming Soon)*

**Affliction Z Series**

*Affliction Z: Patient Zero*

*Affliction Z: Abandoned Hope*

*Affliction Z: Descended in Blood*

*Affliction Z : Fractured Part 1*

*Affliction Z: Fractured Part 2 (Fall 2021)*

Get your very own L.T. Ryan merchandise today! Click the link below to find coffee mugs, t-shirts, and even signed copies of your favorite thrillers! https://ltryan.ink/EvG_

Receive a free copy of The Recruit. Visit:

https://ltryan.com/jack-noble-newsletter-signup-1

# ABOUT THE AUTHOR

L.T. Ryan is a *USA Today* and international bestselling author. The new age of publishing offered L.T. the opportunity to blend his passions for creating, marketing, and technology to reach audiences with his popular Jack Noble series.

Living in central Virginia with his wife, the youngest of his three daughters, and their three dogs, L.T. enjoys staring out his window at the trees and mountains while he should be writing, as well as reading, hiking, running, and playing with gadgets. See what he's up to at http://ltryan.com.

**Social Medial Links:**

- Facebook (L.T. Ryan): https://www.facebook.com/LTRyanAuthor

- Facebook (Jack Noble Page): https://www.facebook.com/JackNobleBooks/

- Twitter: https://twitter.com/LTRyanWrites

- Goodreads: http://www.goodreads.com/author/show/6151659.L_T_Ryan